Now You Wanna Come Back

Now You Wanna
Come Back

Anna Black

www.urbanbooks.net

Urban Books, LLC
300 Farmingdale Road, NY-Route 109
Farmingdale, NY 11735

Now You Wanna Come Back

ISBN 13: 978-1-64556-098-2
ISBN 10: 1-64556-098-8

First Mass Market Printing September 2020
First Trade Paperback Printing April 2020
Printed in the United States of America

10 9 8 7 6 5 4 3 2 1

Distributed by Kensington Publishing Corp.
Submit Orders to:
Customer Service
400 Hahn Road
Westminster, MD 21157-4627
Phone: 1-800-733-3000
Fax: 1-800-659-2436

Now You Wanna Come Back

Anna Black

Hi, readers. Hi, readers, I'm Anna Black, national bestselling author of *I'm Doin' Me* and *Sometimes I'm In My Feelings*. I am originally from the south side of Chicago. I am a divorced mother of one. I now reside in Texas with my 20-year-old daughter, Tyra, who attends Sam Houston State University, and my two dogs, Jaxson and Jasmine.

Professionally, I am in hotel management and have been in my field for twenty years. I enjoy writing, as you all know, and I read as much as time allows. My favorite things are football, playing pool, and crocheting. When I'm not working on a project or on hotel business, I binge watch series on Netflix and Hulu.

I truly enjoyed writing this story about Leila, Rayshon, and Devon, and I hope you guys enjoyed reading it. Please do me a huge favor by spreading the word, leave a review, and check out my other novels, anthologies, and novellas.

Chapter One

I know you see this rock on my finger, Leila thought as she handed her customer his bank card. He had come into her bookstore about an hour ago to purchase literature on healthy eating. Yes, he was fine and had a killer body, but she was in no mood to deal with his arrogant ass.

He walked around the store confidently, no doubt because he knew he was drop-dead gorgeous, but as soon as he opened his mouth, he became a drop-dead gorgeous asshole. He went on and on about himself and how he was this well-known personal trainer in the Chicago area. Of course, Leila, a size-sixteen mother of an adorable 3-month-old little girl, did not have any knowledge of who or what he was, nor did she care. Although he meant no harm and probably wasn't the egotistical asshole she perceived him to be, the sound of his confident voice made insecure Leila want to scream.

She showed him the health section, which was in the back of the store, and made a huge mistake by telling Mr. Physical to let her know if he needed any help. She went back to her stool behind the counter and had opened the novel she was reading when he asked his first question. She got up, walked over, grabbed the book he had asked her about—which sat right in front of his face—and handed it to him.

If it had been a snake, he'd have been bitten, that was for sure. She shook her head as she walked away. Question number two came before she got back to the counter, which caused her to stop in her tracks. She turned her attention back to him and satisfied him with an answer. He followed up with another question. And another. After question number fifteen, she referred him to the internet. She had a nice computer setup in a quiet corner of her store to allow customers to look up material on their own.

That setup was a lifesaver for her on the days she worked alone and days like this . . . *when annoying-ass customers won't leave me the hell alone,* she thought as she sat back behind the counter. The store was empty for a Saturday, and she took advantage of it by catching up on some of her reading. It was usually a madhouse, but since the day was slow, she had sent her staff home. Putting her nose back into her book, she prayed he would get what he needed and bounce. It was getting good, and she didn't want to stop reading.

He finally made his way to the counter with only one book to purchase. *After all those damn questions.* "Will this be all?" Leila asked him when he handed over his card.

"Yes, and your number would be nice."

"Ump, ump," she said, clearing her throat. She handed him his card and then held up her hand to show him her ring. She wondered how he hadn't noticed the bling on her finger, because the lighting in her store made the dazzling gem sparkle so well it could be blinding.

"Aw, my bad. I didn't realize that was a wedding ring," he said. His tone implied her stone wasn't all that.

"Yes, it is," she said sharply.

"Oh, excuse me. I do apologize, Miss Lady."

"It's okay. You have a nice day." She handed him his bag.

He stood there for a moment like he was waiting for something more, then said, "Hey, Leila." She wore a name tag, but he was about the only one who pronounced her name correctly. Most called her "Leela," and it was pronounced "Layla." "My name is Rayshon Johnson, but mostly everyone calls me Ray. Here's my card. If you are ever in need of a physical fitness trainer, hit me up. I'll give you a good deal." He gave her one of his cards.

She took it, looked at it quickly, and put it with a stack of business cards that had been left by other customers for her mailing list but not for anything personal. She would never call him for anything other than book or event info. In fact, it would be sent to his email.

"Well, Rayshon, I thank you for your offer, but as you can see, I don't do gyms, nor do I do physical trainers. Have a nice day," she said with a wink.

"You think only fit people have trainers?"

"Are you implying I'm not fit?" That time she spoke with much attitude.

"No, no, I'm not. You're are a thick sista, and that's fine by me." He leaned on the counter. "You look damn good, and I'm not trying to make you skinny. I just wanna help you to be healthy, so please don't take it offensively. Personally, I prefer a heavier sista, but at the same time, I want my woman eating right and putting in some type of cardio. Even if it's only thirty minutes a day, it all helps for a healthier heart." He sounded caring, not like the "I'm too sexy for my shirt" asshole he'd come into the store as, Leila thought.

"I'm good. If ever the day comes when my husband and I wanna hire a personal trainer, you'll be the first one we call," she said.

His bright smile changed to a look of defeat. He eased back from the counter and backed up a bit. "All right. You take care and tell that husband of yours that he is a lucky man."

"I sure will," Leila said as Rayshon walked out of the door. "Yeah, I'll tell him whenever I get a chance to have a conversation with him again," Leila said out loud once he was on the other side of the door.

Chapter Two

Leila stood on her porch and waited for Devon to get out of his car and bring Deja to her. He worked Monday through Friday and had her on Saturdays so Leila could work at her store. During the workweek, Deja went to Emoni's daycare center a few blocks down from the bookstore. That made it convenient for Leila, and she was comfortable with taking her there.

When she got home, she'd hoped he'd come a little later so she could get some things done around the house, but Devon acted like he had such a busy social life and had to bring the baby right after the bookstore closed. She hadn't been in the house for two minutes before he was blowing his horn in the driveway.

He walked up the steps and handed Deja to Leila in her car seat without a "hello" or "good evening." He was too busy with the conversation that he was having on his Bluetooth to say hello. Leila figured the call was too important for him to pause to simply say hi.

"Yeah, yeah. Hey, hold on a sec," he said to the person he was on the phone with. "She just ate about forty-five minutes ago," he told Leila. "She was grunting in the car on the way, so she may need a new diaper." He turned and walked away.

"And how are you, Devon?" Leila asked.

"I'm fine," he said and kept walking. He proceeded to talk to his Bluetooth as he got back into his Jaguar and pulled out of the driveway. Leila stood on the porch with the baby and diaper bag and watched his taillights go down the street.

She had only been married for six years, and as soon as she got pregnant, Devon made an exit. Not because of the baby and responsibilities, but because he was no longer interested in her. It started out subtle at first, but it didn't take Devon long before he got his own place. First, it was staying out super late, and then it turned into not coming home at all. By her third month, she was on her own. The day Deja was born, Devon swore he would get his act together and come home, but that was three months ago. Three months of lying, false hope, and fake promises.

He took care of them financially, with no fuss, and made sure everything was paid. She never had to ask for this or that, because money had never been an issue with him. The problem with Devon was the in and out. One minute he was in and wanted to make it work, and the next minute he was out. Finally, after all the drama, he told Leila that he was going to file for divorce. But she had yet to see that happen.

Leila didn't even flinch when he said the word "divorce." It had been almost two years since she had even considered them husband and wife. She had already cried all she could cry, prayed all she could pray, and pleaded all she could plead for him to come back to her and for them to be a family again.

She still loved and wanted her husband, yes, but she finally had come to terms with knowing that they were over. She had stopped wishing and hoping, and she'd started setting the alarm on her security system at night with her new code. She wasn't hurting financially at all, because Devon did support her and Deja, and even if he didn't, her mother had left her a nice piece of change when she passed three years ago.

Leila worked in the editing department at a publishing company before she purchased the store. She always had a love of reading, and after her mom died, she took some of her money and opened herself a little bookstore. It wasn't as busy as a Barnes & Noble or an Amazon, but she did well.

And Devon wasn't what one would call poor either. He was a senior partner at a cellular company, and he was pretty much set. At times, she wished he were broke so he could at least need her for her money, but that was not the case. Even her having his first and only child didn't make him want to be with her.

They had met in college and dated forever. After they married, things were good for the most part, but after a few pounds here and a few pounds there, he changed. He didn't want to take Leila out anymore, and the more depressed her marriage made her, the more weight she put on.

When she got pregnant, that really turned him off. He made comments to her at the beginning like, "Man, now you're really going to blow up." He had even asked the doctor, "How much weight does a baby actually put on a woman, generally?" Leila wanted to slap him. She knew she was not the size ten he'd married, but she thought she was still pretty.

"What's your problem?" she'd asked him that day when they got in the car.

"My problem is you not wanting to go to the gym and how you act like you don't realize you're not looking the way you did on our wedding day. That is my problem. You are tipping the scale, Lei, and you act like you don't see how big you have gotten." His voice had been cold, but she had gotten used to him being insulting. It had become the norm.

"I'm pregnant," she'd said in her own defense.

"Only six or seven weeks. That thirty or forty pounds you have gained since we got married has nothing to do with this pregnancy."

"Don't you think I know I'm not a size ten anymore? But I'm not some fat, ugly beast, and I am tired of you acting like you are so disgusted or ashamed of me. You don't have a problem with my weight when you wanna get some. My weight doesn't seem to bother you then. When you wanna please your dick, my weight doesn't seem to stop you from jumping on top of me."

"Oh, so I'm not supposed to want to touch you either?"

"That's not what I mean, Devon. If you love me enough to still wanna make love to me, you should love me enough to still wanna take me out with you, or wanna spend more time with me and not always put me down. You never hold me anymore. You don't take me places like you used to, and I am so tired of you making insulting remarks about me. If you loved me, you wouldn't do that," she had said, crying.

"Well, maybe I don't," he'd said callously.

"What? Maybe you don't what?" she'd asked, hoping he didn't mean what she thought he was saying.

"Love you," he'd said.

Leila's heart had dropped. "What?" she'd asked softly.

He hadn't said another word.

After that, things got worse. He slowly moved out, and Leila cried herself to sleep every night. She woke up every morning wishing she had never married him. He was the only man she'd ever loved, and his love was conditional. When he'd visit his daughter, he'd look at Leila with this look of disappointment. It got to where she hated to be in the same room with him, so she'd make it a point to have something to run out to do, or she'd make herself busy in another room to avoid him altogether.

When he told her about his plans to file for a divorce, she simply said, "So be it." She would just somehow move on and just focus on her business and her baby girl. Hell, maybe she'd even love again. She had no clue, but what she did know was she wasn't going to keep hoping for her and Devon to work things out.

Inside, she sat the baby in her carrier on the table and put the diaper bag on a chair. "Hey, sweetie pie. How ya doing, girl?" she asked as she unstrapped her daughter and picked her up. Deja smiled beautifully, the nub of a tooth poking through her gumline. "Aw, I see how you are doing, stinky girl," Leila said, walking her up to the nursery. She took her over to her changing table and strapped her down, then went into the hall bathroom and started the water. She put the baby tub into the big tub and filled it with warm water.

She went back into the nursery to undress her little doll. "There we go, baby. Let's get this stinky stuff off my baby."

Deja laughed and kicked her little legs while Leila gave her a bath and shampooed her hair. After she put lotion on her, she sat in her rocker to nurse her.

"I guess it's you and me, kid, again on a lonely Saturday night," Leila said sadly. After Deja burped, she put her down in her crib.

Deja was a good baby, so she was content while Leila did a few things around the house. She went back to check on her, and she was sleeping. Leila checked her diaper, and although she hated to change her while she was sleeping, she had to. She made it through the diaper change without disturbing the baby too badly, and she fell right back to sleep.

It was only eight o'clock, and Leila was bored. She went downstairs and looked through all of her DVDs to find something to watch, but out of 800 movies, she couldn't find one she felt like watching.

She went back to her room and climbed into bed and picked up the remote to her television. She flipped through the channels and landed on *The Cosby Show*. *How can Clair and Cliff be so happy?* she wondered. "Maybe because Clair never got fat," she said to herself and muted the volume. She grabbed her book and picked up where she left off.

Once she got deep into it, her phone rang. It was Devon. She looked at the clock and saw it was after nine. *What in the hell does he want?* she wondered.

"Hello," she answered wryly.

"Hey, Lei, this is Devon."

"I know. What is it?"

"Well, I got DJ's binky, and I'm going to bring it back for you," he said.

Leila rolled her eyes and thought, *you've got to be kidding me*. "Devon, Deja has three or four binkies around here. Besides, she's already asleep."

"Are you sure? I'm only about five minutes away."

"I'm sure. We're good."

"Well, let me come by anyway so I can see her."

"Devon, what are you . . . Are you on drugs? She is asleep. Did you not hear me say that?"

"Okay, I'll be there in five." He hung up before Leila could argue. She got up and put on a pair of sweats. She had on a tank, too, but didn't bother to change it because it was only Devon. Her hair was pulled back, and she had on her glasses, but she didn't attempt to fix herself up for him. The doorbell rang as she was walking down the stairs.

She opened the door, and he was standing there with the binky in his hand.

"Thanks," she said and took it from him. She walked away, and he followed her inside and closed the door.

"Where's DJ?" he asked.

She cocked her head to the left and looked at him. "Are you slow? Where do you think? She is in her crib." She put as much attitude in her voice as she could.

She walked into the kitchen, and he followed right behind her. She poured herself a glass of juice, not offering him anything.

"She could have been in her bassinet or in our bed. I don't know," he said.

"She is not in my bed. She is in her crib," she said. He was irritating her, and she made it known by rolling her eyes at him. *What's with the "our bed" madness?* He hadn't lived there in months.

"I'm going to go up and see her."

"Go ahead," Leila said.

She sat on the sofa and didn't bother to follow him up. She grabbed the remote and turned on the television. She never had any problems with Devon seeing Deja and never denied him the opportunity to come over if he wanted to spend time with her. But why was he trying to see her when he knew she was sleeping?

After a little while, she wondered what was taking him so long to come back down. She put the remote down and went up to see what he was doing. Maybe he'd woken Deja up and was just holding her. When she reached the top of the steps, she went into the nursery. No Devon. She tapped on the hall bathroom, and no one answered.

She went back to look in on Deja. The baby was still in her crib, sleeping peacefully. Leila walked slowly down the hall to her bedroom, and she knew she was going to have to cuss his ass out.

"No, no, no. Get the hell up outta my bed, Negro," she yelled. "You think you're slick, but I'm not having it tonight."

She had vowed he'd never touch her again unless they were going to get back together, and here he was pulling another move on her like she had STUPID written across her forehead.

"I need you tonight," he said with his puppy-dog eyes.

"You can't be serious," she said, trying to keep a straight face.

"Why wouldn't I be? Lei, I love you, and you know that. Things are just difficult right now between us, but I never fell out of love with you. I was just so attracted to the woman I married, and you changed. You changed," he said sadly.

"My exterior changed, yes, but I am the same woman you married. That is not an excuse for you to walk out on me. I am sick and tired of you treating me like your doormat. You can't come over here whenever you feel like you wanna screw me and expect me to get all excited for you."

"That's not it. Do you think I don't miss you? Do you think I don't love you? I've never stopped loving you."

"Then why aren't you here?" she yelled. He didn't respond. He sat there and didn't say a word. "Exactly," she said. She walked over to her side of the bed and sat down.

He moved closer to her. "Lei, please. I don't want to upset you. I just want you to understand. I'm still in love with you, but I wish I had the old you."

"Well, you can't have any of the new me tonight," she said and got up.

"Can I at least stay the night, please? I'm tired, and I don't want to be by myself tonight. I'll get up with the baby and give you a break. Just let me stay. I don't feel like driving to the other side of town tonight."

"Fine, you can stay. But don't touch me. And you betta get your ass up with Deja, too. I'm not playing with you."

She went downstairs to turn everything off and set the alarm, then went to shower. After she moisturized her skin, she climbed into bed and drifted off to sleep. Of course, as the night progressed, their bodies made contact, and the feeling of his hardness pressed against her ass made it hard to resist his moves.

Before she could fight it or protest his advances, Devon was deep inside of her, doing what she didn't want him to do, while she moaned and panted. It felt good to have him inside of her, and she wished it wasn't a temporary situation. By the time he was done working her body over, she was exhausted.

He did what he said he would do by taking care of the baby when she got up for her feeding, allowing Leila to sleep. The next morning, he fixed breakfast and hung around, and they played husband and wife for a few hours. It was temporary, as usual, and he made his normal exit around two that afternoon.

Leila shut the door behind him and hated herself for allowing him to have his way with her. She wanted to be over him and completely done, but he was her only source of dick, so she put up with him when she needed to. The times she was okay and didn't need the attention, she'd shut Devon down with a quickness, but last night wasn't one of those times. She let her body have its own way.

She went upstairs to get Deja and went into her bedroom. She saw Devon had conveniently forgotten his watch on the nightstand of what used to be his side of the bed. For some reason, she couldn't figure out why, he still had a lot of his stuff there, even though he had a condo on the other side of town. Many times, Leila would promise herself she'd gather his stuff and box it all up, but time had gone by, and she still hadn't done it. She took the watch and placed it inside the top drawer of his nightstand, where she normally put all the personal items he left behind after their rendezvous. He'd always say, "I'll get it next time," but somehow, next time hadn't come around yet.

The day rolled by, and by nightfall, Leila was sad that Devon had gotten her goods and totally ignored her the rest of the day. She fought the urge to call him after she put Deja down for the night. "It's okay, DJ. We are gonna be fine without him," she said.

Her sweet, innocent infant had no clue of how messed up things were. She was too small to see that her parents were not together and had so many issues. If she knew how much pain her momma was in, she'd probably hate her daddy. The thought made Leila relieved that she was still a baby.

When Leila got into bed, she closed her eyes and thanked God for giving her such a good baby. She knew she was fortunate. People had told her that if you cry a lot during your pregnancy, your baby will be a crybaby. Leila knew for a fact that that myth was a lie, because although she tried her hardest not to, she cried a lot during her entire pregnancy and Deja was not a crybaby.

She made sure the baby monitor was on before she got ready to go to sleep, and then she decided to try Devon before she called it a night. Of course, she got his voicemail and didn't bother to leave him a message. She texted him and, as she expected, never got a response. She didn't get angry at all because she was accustomed to his behavior. She got into bed and fell asleep easily.

The two a.m. baby alarm was right on schedule. Deja was up for her feeding. Even if the monitor didn't work, Leila could hear her crying from a mile away. Leila dragged herself out of bed and went to take care of her baby.

It was hard, but in the end, it was all worth it.

Chapter Three

"Ten, nine, eight, seven, six, five, come on, three, two, and one. Good job," Rayshon said to his client. He really hated this session, but it was the best-paying session he had. Christa was a gorgeous, vanilla-complexioned woman with dots here and there on her skin that people referred to as beauty marks. Ray only saw them as moles. She had been his client for four years and had referred tons of her model friends to him.

She was five feet nine inches and didn't have more than 1 percent of body fat on her toned body. She had long, wavy hair that she sometimes wore blown out straight. She was of mixed race, Korean and black, and told Rayshon that she was always teased, called a war baby because her daddy was in the military and had married a Korean woman. Although no wars were going on when she was conceived, she was always teased with the same joke.

Ray liked her and admired her beauty, but he didn't like her romantically. Although she was gorgeous, she had much attitude. There was nothing humble about her. She would always flirt with him and make comments about how she could get any man she wanted. She was a bitch to the tenth power, and she would not stop her quest to get with him, so he couldn't stand to be around her most of the time.

She even went so far as to say he was gay. She told one of the girls she referred that he had to be a down-low brother if he didn't want her, which was 100 percent wrong. Ray loved women, and he was as masculine as they came, inside and out. From his head to his toes, he was the epitome of manly.

He just had one rule of business—never date any of his clients. Dating a client or a coworker, to him, was the worst thing for anyone's business. Just like word of mouth, it could either build your business or annihilate your business, bringing referrals or having a client you made a big mistake hooking up with ruin your business's name because things didn't go their way. Christa was one of those types of clients who would bring a brother's business down.

Lucky for him, he provided his clients with that top-notch service and didn't have to work anymore as an employee at the gym where he had started. He could now come and go as he pleased according to his schedule and his appointments. He was set up at home, and things were marvelous, so he had no intention of dating any of his clients.

Because Christa was a local model and did a lot of work in the Chicago area, she looked down on most. She had a li'l clout, and her head was swollen. She was recognized everywhere she went, and she believed the hype, so she preferred to work out at Ray's loft. He had converted his upstairs into a training area. He had a treadmill, elliptical, bike, free weights, a bench, jump ropes, mats, and bands. It was a private and profitable setup, but he hated having her and a couple other clients there alone because it never failed that they thought they could seduce him.

Christa met with Ray at least four times a week and didn't have a set schedule due to her so-called career, so she made her appointments weekly according to her schedule and his availability. She paid more for flex scheduling, and they were both happy with their arrangement. The only thing that made Ray unhappy was the constant flirting. She'd try him every session, and he'd turn her down every time. If it had not been for the good money, heavy referrals, and the fact that they had a contract, he would have let her go a long time ago. Since his goal was to open his own fitness center one day, he put up with a lot of shit that he didn't want to tolerate.

"I'll see you Wednesday?" Ray asked, walking Christa to the door. Her session had run a couple minutes over, and he only had ten minutes to prepare for his next client.

"Yes, Wednesday." She smiled seductively and moved closer to him. "Or if you'd like to see me sooner . . ."

He knew she was on a mission to break him down because, according to what she had told him, he was the first and only man she'd ever met who didn't try to sleep with her.

"Christa, we do this every session. I told you I don't date my clients," he said, backing up.

"Well, I don't wanna be your client anymore."

"Yes, you do," he said, smiling.

"No, I don't. You're fired. Now let's go and get this over with," she said, reaching for him.

He stopped her dead in her tracks. "Well, Ms. Thang, you can't fire me because we have a contract. And because you know I'm the best," he boasted.

"Damn, Ray, why are you so stubborn?" She rubbed the tip of her fingers down the center of her chest. "You know you want this."

"Bye, Christa. I've gotta get ready for my next session."

"All right, Mr. Do the Right Thing. You gon' give in to me sooner or later. I know you wanna taste this," she said, smiling.

Ray walked her to the door. "Well, until then, I'll see you on Wednesday," he said and closed the door behind her. She was fine, and he could tap that ass right, but he didn't want to go there with her. He didn't want a woman like Christa. She'd be more than a handful, and he didn't want a relationship with or to be involved with a woman he knew one day he may want to shake the shit out of.

He wiped the equipment down with the sanitizing wipes and dashed to the door to open it for Loran. She was one of the chicks Christa had referred to him. She was just as bad, but he knew how to handle their asses. He let her in, and they got started right away. She had a nice body and was a dime, but she always wore a weave.

Ray didn't understand why sistas always had to have a weave. He really hated his clients, who always complained about sweating their weave out. He'd heard it a million times, and it drove him insane. How did they expect to lose weight and get in shape without sweating? That was one of his things: he couldn't date a woman with weave.

After Loran's session, he had two more clients to see before he had some free time. Once he was done with his morning sessions, he showered and decided he'd run back to the bookstore to get the other book that he should have gotten before. He knew he should have gotten it, but he didn't remember why he didn't.

He pulled his Tahoe into a parking space and noticed a sign on the door that read, BE BACK IN fIfTEEN MINUTES. He sat in his truck and waited. A few moments later, a gray Armada pulled into the private parking space on the side of the building. A woman got out, and he saw it was Leila. She looked kind of different, he thought. She didn't have on glasses, she had on makeup, and her hair was down. She was actually pretty, he thought while he checked her out. He waited until she got inside before he got out.

She took the sign down, and he watched through the huge glass window as she walked to the counter, imagining he could sculpt her thick body to perfection if given a chance. He would give her definition in her arms while leaving her perfect breasts the way they were. She'd be a showstopper. He got out of his SUV and walked into the store.

The bell on the door alerted Leila that someone had come in. "I'll be with you in a moment," she yelled from the back.

Ray walked over to the counter and saw his card on top of the stack of business cards. *At least she didn't throw it away,* he thought when she came out of the back office.

"I'm sorry to have kept you waiting," she said.

"Hey, Leila," he said and smiled.

"Oh, it's you again. Hi, how are you?" she asked.

Ray wondered what was going on with her because she returned the warm smile that he had given her. "I'm good," he said. "I just wanted to come by and pick up that other book you recommended."

"Okay, I can get that for you." She came from behind the counter, and he followed her. "Here you are," she said, handing it to him. "This is the right one, isn't it?"

"Yes, this is it."

"Is there anything else you'd like me to get for you?"

"There is, actually," he said.

"And that is?" she asked impatiently.

"I know you said that you weren't interested in hiring a personal trainer, but what if I gave you a session for free? I mean, you can't beat free. And if you don't have a good time and don't feel motivated to come again, I'll leave you alone."

"No," she said, walking away. "Not interested."

"What do you mean, no? It's a free session, and trust me, my love, my sessions are not cheap."

"No, thank you," she said, folding her arms across her ample breasts.

"What's the big deal? It's a free session. It'll be fun. I mean, what do you have to lose?"

"What is your problem?" she growled.

He could see she was losing patience. "Hold on. I don't have a problem. I was just trying to offer you something that might change your life."

"What is with you guys? Am I just that disgusting to look at that I must get to the gym right now? What if I like how I look? Why are people so worried about a woman's size? We are not all skinny, okay? We can't all look like Beyoncé," she yelled.

"Listen, I'm sorry, okay? I wasn't trying to offend you or imply that you need to lose weight. I see women all day in various shapes and sizes, and trust me, I know y'all can't all look like Beyoncé. I understand that some women have problem areas, and no matter how hard you work at it, it will never achieve the look you want. I understand that some things are not physically possible to achieve with diet and exercise. You are a very attractive woman, and I'd be a fool if I saw you out and didn't notice you. I'm sorry if I offended you. I'm in business to help people, not just women, get healthy and get into shape.

"Not all of my clients are skinny, and I haven't come across a Beyoncé yet. Not naturally anyway," he said jokingly and smiled. "They've been nipped and tucked here and there," he said, and the tension in her face loosened. "You are fine just the way you are, and I'm not here to make you lose weight. I just wanna motivate you to have a healthier heart. If you work with me only thirty minutes with cardio alone, that will change your life. And your husband's," he said, trying to make her feel comfortable.

"Look, I understand what you are trying to say. I'm just a little sore right now. I didn't mean to snap off on you like that." She gave him a little smile.

"Don't sweat it. I'm cool." He stared at her.

"What? Why are you looking at me like that?"

"I would be better if you would just try one session," he tried again. "Not commit yourself, but just try one. I know you'd love it."

"Okay, Rayshon, maybe one. I can't guarantee you anything. but I may give it a try."

"You have my card, and as I said before, your husband too. It's a lot of fun for couples to do it together. My married clients have a blast."

"I may, but I can't say my husband will." Her smile faded. "As a matter of fact, I'm sure he won't. We don't do stuff like that together."

Ray didn't want to pry, so he didn't ask why not. "That's cool. You coming alone will be fun as well. Just give me a call so we can set something up."

"I will," she said and proceeded to ring up the book. "Maybe if I have fun, I'll sign up."

"I'll have your contract ready because I know you are gonna wanna come back."

"Hold on, Rayshon. You are getting ahead of yourself."

"Oh, my bad," he said, taking the bag she held out.

"Thanks for stopping in. Keep us in mind for your next book purchase," she said.

"I most definitely will, and I hope to hear from you soon," he said, and he left.

Chapter Four

"Come on, Devon," Leila said, looking at her watch. It was five 'til eight, and Devon was twenty-five minutes late. She had plans to go to the movies with her girlfriend Renee, and Devon was supposed to keep the baby for her. Since the next day was Saturday and she had to open the store, he had agreed to keep the baby all night.

He finally pulled into the driveway, and Leila almost passed out when she saw a woman in the passenger seat. He had never gone so far as to bring someone to her house with him before, and her fists instantly balled up at her sides.

Leila could see the young woman clearly. Devon had parked under the bright sensor light that was attached to her garage. She was pretty, and she was definitely slim. Very petite. That made Leila even madder.

"Who in the hell is that?" she asked between clenched teeth, not trying to bring attention to herself. She wanted to slap the piss out of him

for bringing some female with him to her house
to pick up their daughter.

"Don't even trip. She's a coworker," he replied.
"Our meeting ran over, and since I was running
late, I had to swing by here to get Deja before
I took her back to her car." He tried to take the
baby's carrier out of Leila's hand, but she held
on tight.

"Don't lie to me. I'm not stupid."

"Lei, please give me the baby and calm yourself
down. You can come and meet her if you like."

"I don't wanna meet that trick. Do you know
how many mistresses smile in women's faces
and fuck their husbands behind their backs?"
Leila asked, raising her voice. She wanted Devon
to know that she wasn't stupid.

"You're insane, you know that? I will talk to
you later."

"Later when?" she asked, still not releasing the
tight grip she had on the baby's carrier.

"Don't make a scene. Come to the car. You
can meet her. She works in our accounting
department. I wouldn't disrespect you like that,
Lei. You know I'm not that foolish."

She knew his ass was lying, but she let the
carrier go, straightened up her face, and walked
out to the car. "Hi, I'm Leila, Devon's wife."

"Hello, Leila, I'm Michelle. I've heard a lot about you," the woman said.

Leila wondered exactly what Devon had told her. "Have you?" Leila looked at Devon out of the corner of her eye.

"Yes. On the ride over here, Devon was telling me what a wonderful mother you are and about your bookstore." She smiled.

Leila had a strong feeling that she was full of shit and that that wasn't all Devon had told her. "Did he?"

"Yeah, and I'd love to check out your store. I mean, I love to read."

The other woman had a huge smile on her beautiful face, and Leila was crumbling on the inside. "Well, whenever you wanna stop in . . . We are open every day except Sundays."

"I will," Michelle said.

Leila saw that Devon was done strapping the baby in. "It was nice to meet you, Michelle."

"You too."

Leila knew the woman's smile was fake and that she was sucking Devon's dick. "All right, Devon, I'll call you tonight to check on DJ."

"And you enjoy your movie. Tell Renee I said hello." He got in and put his seat belt on.

"Okay, drive safely. And you have a good night, Michelle."

"You too," she said.

Leila frowned at her as Devon put the car in gear. Who was this bitch to call her Lei like she knew her? She backed away from the car to keep from saying another word and watched them drive off with her baby girl. How long had this little five-pound-twelve-ounce bitch been fucking her husband?

She didn't spend much time thinking about Michelle and Devon because it didn't matter. There was nothing she could do to stop Devon from doing what he wanted, so she tried to not think of them. She went inside and called Renee to tell her they would have to catch a later movie. Renee said it would be better to go a different night because she wasn't trying to go that late. Leila hung up, disappointed that they couldn't hang out for a while. She definitely didn't want to be in the house that night.

She went into the bathroom, undressed, and looked at herself. Her reflection made her sad. She was out of shape and fat, she thought. She thought about Michelle, the bombshell in her husband's passenger seat, rolling around with him, and she started to cry.

"That's why you left me?" she yelled at the mirror and sobbed.

She put on her robe, went downstairs, and poured herself a glass of wine. She had pumped enough for a few days so she could enjoy a couple of glasses. She turned on the radio and found herself singing and crying. After her little pity party, she turned off everything, climbed the steps, and went into her bedroom. She climbed into her empty king-sized bed and pulled up the covers.

She picked up the phone and called Devon. He answered on the fifth ring.

"Hey, Lei, what's up?"

"Nothing. How is my baby?"

"She's good. I just put her down about ten minutes ago," he said. Leila heard a voice in the background.

"Who is that?" she demanded.

"Nobody," he said.

"Come on, nobody? Is that Michelle?" she yelled.

"No. I told you—"

"Don't lie to me. Tell me the truth. Are you with Michelle?" she demanded.

"Can we talk about this tomorrow?"

"Hell no. We are still married."

"Please, I have people here," he said, speaking low.

"Oh, so you're entertaining? Why didn't you invite me over? Why wasn't I invited to your little party?" she yelled. She was a little tipsy from the three glasses of wine she drank, and she was upset that he was living the life while she was already in bed by ten on a Friday night. "How are you taking care of Deja and having a party?"

"Listen, I gotta go. My daughter is fine. I am responsible enough to have guests and take care of my child. And it is not a party."

"Why are you doing this to me? I love you so much, and you act like you don't even care," she said, crying.

"Look, Leila, tomorrow. I'll call you tomorrow," he said and hung up.

"Devon. Devon," she said and put the phone down.

She didn't bother calling him back because she knew it wouldn't do any good. She got on her knees and cried until her head ached. She begged God for strength. She just didn't want to hurt anymore. She didn't want to love him anymore. She wanted to be okay with who she was and how she looked. She wanted peace.

She got up, got back into bed, and decided that he wouldn't make her cry herself to sleep again. That was how it had been for her the past couple of years, and crying herself to sleep would come to an end that night.

Chapter Five

The next day, Leila went to work and avoided calling Devon at all costs. She was embarrassed by how she acted on the phone with him, for one, and for two, she didn't want to hear his voice. If he wanted a divorce, she would give him the divorce. She was tired of caring about him or who he was with. She just wanted to focus on herself.

That morning, she had taken off her extravagant wedding ring and put it in her jewelry box. There was no point in faking the funk and walking around claiming to be married to a man who'd left her. She mostly wore it to keep from looking like a single mom when she was by herself with the baby, but now she didn't care what people thought, because she was what she was—a single mom.

She felt free for a change and didn't want to keep walking around being unnoticed and ignored by folks. She set up a hair appointment and decided to get her nails and feet done, too.

It was the third week of August. Fall was around the corner, and she didn't have any cold-weather clothes that fit, so she needed to go shopping. She left Renee at the bookstore and told her she'd be back before closing.

She'd had no idea how hard it would be to find pretty clothes in her size. Every rack she went to made her upset. She remembered when she was small and could just grab what she wanted off the rack and go home without even trying anything on. But those days were gone, and she wondered how plus-size women made it with cute clothes being so limited.

She felt like an outcast and hated having to try on everything. She managed to leave the mall with several things, but it was work. She didn't care, because all she wanted was a start on her new attitude and new look. After she got her hair, nails, and feet done, she felt better.

When she got back to the store, Renee's mouth dropped open. "Wow, girl, you look good. I almost didn't recognize you."

"You think so?"

"Yes, ma'am. I should have gone with you instead of hanging around here all day. I mean, the hair, the makeup, and the new threads . . . You look like a model."

"G'on now, girl," Leila said.

"For real. I should have gone too."

"Were we busy today?"

"Yes and no. We had spurts. Oh, and a fine brother came in here asking about you, Ms. Leila. Told me to tell you that he's still waiting for you to set up that appointment."

Leila knew exactly who she was talking about. "Yeah," she said. She thought about taking him on. She could at least try it.

"And my Lord, he was fine," Renee said.

"He's all right."

"You know who I'm talking about?"

"Yes. His card is right there. He's a personal trainer."

"He can be my personal everything. Shit, girl, he's like . . . damn! I couldn't stop staring. If my husband had been here, he would have snatched my eyeballs out," Renee said, and they laughed.

"He's okay. Devon is finer than he is," Leila said. Her husband was still in her heart.

"Yeah, let you tell it. You're stuck on Devon's behind. If you didn't know Devon and saw them both walking down the street, who would you pick?"

"Devon," Leila said.

"Chile, please, Devon got you hooked."

"No, he doesn't. I don't even like Devon like that anymore. You know we are done."

"I know he is, but are you?"

"Well, we are married."

"Married, but not happily married," Renee said.

"Whatever. You just don't like Devon."

"No, I do like Devon. That is Deja's father. I just don't like the way he treats Deja's mother."

"That's in the past. I'm moving on with my life."

"And you can start by making that appointment."

"That has nothing to do with me moving on."

"I know, but after looking at him for, what, an hour a day, you'll be like, 'Devon who?'" They laughed.

"You are a mess," Leila said and went to lock the door.

She turned off the OPEN sign, and they closed the bookstore. She and Renee were going to see the movie they had missed the night before. Before Leila left the store, she grabbed the card that Rayshon had left and stuck it into her purse.

When Leila got home, she called Devon to let him know it was okay to bring Deja home, but she got his voicemail. She left him a message letting him know she was home, then tried on the outfits again that she had purchased earlier.

She still had on her makeup, and her hair looked good. It was nice and bouncy, and her new highlights complemented her pretty face. She had gotten her brows arched, her eyes were bright, and she was happy for a change.

She stood in the mirror, admiring herself and smiling. She felt like she looked good. She wasn't the same size she used to be, but she was wearing it well. Her vanilla complexion and slightly slanted eyes drew attention to her face. She had smooth skin with only a couple of blemishes from the occasional menstrual breakout, and she didn't require a lot of foundation to cover up.

She had a slim nose with high cheekbones, and her full lips were beautiful with the dark red lipstick she had on. Her natural brown hair always hung past her shoulders, and she was glad she'd made the risky decision to layer it and change the old, boring color. She was checking herself out in a pair of tight jeans and a cream-colored sweater when her doorbell rang. She ran down and looked through the peephole. It was Devon. *Damn, he must have been on his way over when I called.*

She opened the door and saw Devon's jaw drop to the floor. He stood there, staring at her.

"Come on in," she said and walked away. He walked in behind her, and she felt his eyes on her. He put the baby on the table in her carrier and put her bag on the floor.

Leila carried on as if he weren't there. She didn't have anything to say to him. She came into the family room to get her baby, but she was asleep. She took her out of her carrier and started talking to her, trying to wake her, but apparently, Deja was too tired. She put her in the bassinet that was kept downstairs instead of taking her to her nursery.

"Damn, Lei, where you been?"

"To the movies," she said, not stopping to chat.

"With whom?" he asked.

"Excuse me?"

"With whom? You weren't with Renee looking like that. Those jeans are hugging your hips like they were painted on. Normally you're in maternity clothes or in sweats with your hair pulled back with no makeup and wearing glasses. Now you're looking sexy and voluptuous. I know damn well you were not with Renee."

"Why can't I be out with Renee? Because I made an effort today to look human?"

"No, because you look like you're trying to entice a man."

"Well, I am grown and on my own."

"What the hell does that mean?" he yelled.

"It means I am going to start living for me and start worrying about my future, not our future. Your life is going on without me, and I should be going on without you."

"Wait a minute. We are still married."

"That's what I said to you last night, right before you hung up on me. So now I'm living my life for me, Devon. Me," she said, pointing at herself.

"I never said that there was no chance for us to get back together."

"Your lips didn't, but your actions do."

"So now you're out dating, is that it? Some dude done whispered some mack-daddy bullshit in your ear, and now we're done?"

"You got it all wrong. You see, I decided to stop waiting on you to control what I do and who I do it with. If you cared so much, we'd be together under one roof, living as husband and wife, instead of you dropping DJ off. You'd be here for us and here to make me feel like a woman. You told me, 'Fuck you,' the day you forwarded your mail. I will say this so you can understand." She walked closer to him. "The ball is not in your possession anymore. You are not going to score another point with making Leila feel bad, nor will you hurt me again. I am done crying myself to sleep every night. I am done with wishing and praying and hoping. Devon, I am done with you," she said and walked into the kitchen.

"You want a divorce?" he asked, following her.

"No, Devon, I want you. I want my marriage, but I am sick and tired of these games, so if you're not here to tell me we are going to be together and be a family and make our marriage work, this conversation is over."

"Just like that? You have nothing else to say to me?"

"What do you want me to do? I mean, seriously, tell me, what do you suppose I do? You are the one who says you want a divorce, and then you don't file, and then you come back around here, giving me hope that we are going to work it out. What do I do, Devon, huh? I mean, really? Just keep spending my nights alone, wondering when or if my husband is coming home? Do you expect me to really let you keep coming by and getting some ass when you want it and then taking off? Come on, tell me."

"I expect you to act like a mother and give your man a minute to get himself together. Do you think you need to be bringing strange men around my daughter?"

"That's all you're worried about? Another man in my face? Why worry about that? I'm a smart woman and a good mother, and I wouldn't expose my daughter to anything that is not appropriate. Deja is three months old, so please don't go there with that nonsense. You don't have a problem with having my baby around Michelle."

"Michelle is a coworker," he said.

"Yeah, whatever. I know you don't expect me to believe that lie," she hissed. She walked away, and he followed her. She went upstairs to change her clothes.

He watched her take off her pants. "You're wearing a thong?"

"Whatever, Devon." She rolled her eyes, grabbed her robe, and then put it on.

"I see you've been shopping."

"And I see you're still here."

"You're putting me out?"

"You're ridiculous." She tried to walk by him, but he blocked her path. "Move," she said, pushing past him.

"We are not over, Lei."

"Then prove it," she challenged.

"What?"

"If we are not over, go and get your stuff and come home tonight."

"It's not that simple."

"It is that simple." She got in his face. "Get in your car, or better yet, take off your clothes, get in the bed, and get comfortable. In the morning, we'll get up, have breakfast, and go get your things. Then we take it one day at a time, and we make our marriage work."

"I want to, but—"

She didn't let him finish. "Then we are over. Please show yourself out."

"Lei, baby. Please—"

She went into the bathroom and shut the door. She hadn't shed one tear and was determined not to let him see her cry. She came out of the bathroom and walked around, totally ignoring his efforts to talk to her.

He finally grabbed his keys and headed for the door. "I love you, Lei," he said.

She didn't feel a thing. His words were just words with no meaning behind them. He stood in the doorway for a few moments, and she got her baby and went up the stairs. She didn't go back down to lock the door until she heard his car pull out of the driveway.

Chapter Six

After cleaning her house and doing a few loads of laundry, Leila decided that she and Deja would get dressed and go out for a while. She had no particular place she wanted to go, but she didn't want to be in the house. She dressed her baby first and went into her room and made herself look glamorous for their outing. She was used to being in the house for the entire day on Sundays, so she was excited to be up and dressed and getting out of the house.

She got in the truck and decided they'd go to the park and then to the mall. She was smiling when she put on her shades because she felt like a sexy mom. She admired her reflection in the rearview mirror. Her hair was fresh, and she'd managed to do her makeup well. She cranked the engine and turned to look over her shoulder to pull out. Then she remembered that her baby's stroller was with Devon.

She wanted to avoid him at all costs, but God wasn't making it easy on her. To walk in the park or through the mall, she had to have the stroller. She got on the main road and headed toward Devon's condo. She didn't bother calling because she didn't want to even hear his voice. When she got there, there was a two-seat BMW in his guest parking stall, so she parked in the stall across from it because she knew she'd only be a minute.

She got to his floor, walked down the hall, and rang the bell of his unit. When the door opened, she wished she had called first. It was Michelle, and she didn't look like she was dressed for work, but Leila kept her cool. She had known she was with Devon from the moment she met her.

"Umm, hi, umm, Lei. How . . . how ya doing?" Michelle said nervously.

"I'm fine, and you?"

"I'm good. I was on my way out. I just stopped by to pick up some papers."

"Where's Devon? I need my baby's stroller," Leila said. She wasn't even trying to go in. She had her baby in her arms, and she knew getting crazy would only frighten her.

"Hold on." Michelle went toward the hallway that led to the bedroom and called out Devon's name.

He came out in a pair of shorts and no shirt. His reaction was one of a shocked man, seeing the person he had just lied to about his status with Michelle. Leila didn't comment.

"Lei, hey. Come in."

Leila could see he was nervous. He was doing a horrible job of trying to play it cool.

He rushed over to the door. "Hey, Deja, how is daddy's baby girl?" He grabbed the baby's little hand, and she started to smile at her daddy. "Come in, Lei. Why are you standing in the door?"

"I just need to get DJ's stroller," Leila said. She mentally congratulated herself for doing an awesome job of not crying. She wasn't hurt. She was too tired and emotionally drained to even react to the situation.

"Sure, let me . . ." He scrambled for his keys.

"You might wanna grab a shirt, lover man. And, Michelle, it was good seeing you again." Leila turned to walk away before the other woman could respond. She overheard Devon asking her why she opened the door and Michelle saying she didn't know it was Leila, that she thought it was the delivery guy with their food.

Devon was down in a matter of minutes to get the stroller, trying to explain.

"Save it, Devon, I don't care to hear it. Just get the stroller, man," Leila told him while she put Deja in her car seat.

"Trust me, nothing is going on up there. I promise it's not what you think," he said.

More lies. Would he ever tell her the truth? He put the stroller in the back of Leila's Armada.

"I don't care. I am drained. You've sucked every ounce of energy out of me. Just go back upstairs to your 'nothing,' so I can take my baby to the park," she said and got into the truck.

"Lei, baby, I love you. I swear, I love you, and I love Deja. I want you and I want DJ. So, please, just bear with me and let me work this out."

"No. Please, Devon, don't do any favors for me. Go back and spend time with Michelle. That's what you want."

"It's work, that's it." He looked sincere, but Leila knew his eyes and lips were lying.

"Yes, I'm sure you're working hard to please someone other than your wife," Leila said and shut the door. Devon tapped on the window, but Leila cranked her truck and put it in gear to pull out. He stood there looking at her, and she waved her hand, motioning for him to step back. He hesitated but finally stepped back.

Leila drove away, telling herself not to cry, but the tears burned her eyes, and she couldn't control them. She decided to go back home. She had confronted the reality that she really had to move on. She and Devon were honestly over and he and Michelle were an item.

At home, she fed Deja and put her in her swing, then undressed and cleaned the makeup from her face. She knew Devon knew the jig was up because he was calling and texting her cell phone every ten minutes. She looked in the mirror, and the image of petite, sexy Michelle opening the door and looking like a black Barbie doll made her angry. She sobbed and wished she hadn't changed. She wished her figure was still the one she had six years ago when she and Devon got married.

She went downstairs and grabbed the ice cream out of the freezer and got a spoon. She sat on the sofa and cried and ate the ice cream. She stood up to go upstairs to check on her baby, and she accidentally knocked her purse over. All of her belongings fell on the floor. She set the ice cream on the coffee table and started to put the items back into her purse. She stopped when she picked up Rayshon's card. She looked at the ice cream and decided to give him a call.

Chapter Seven

"Hi, this is Ray," Rayshon said when he answered.

"Hello, Rayshon. This is Leila from the bookstore," she said nervously.

"Hey, Leila. How's it going?"

"Okay, I guess," she said.

"You don't sound too good. What's wrong? You sound down."

"I'm fine, just had a bad day."

"I feel you. I've had one a time or two."

"Yeah, I've had them a lot here lately."

"Don't sweat it. Things don't stay bad for long."

"I guess."

"I take it you're finally calling to set up that session?"

"Yes, you are correct."

"That's great. When did you wanna start?"

"Well, I don't know. How early or how late do you take appointments?"

"That depends if you want to meet at the gym or at my loft."

"What's the difference?"

"My mornings are done here at my loft, and late evenings I sometimes meet clients at the gym. Time slots vary in cost, and my prices are different for early mornings and late evenings. If you aren't signing up for a gym membership, you'll have to come here anyway, because all my clients I see at the gym have a membership there."

"Okay, so what's the earliest and what's the latest?"

"The earliest is five a.m., and the latest is nine p.m. It depends on what works best for the client and what is open for scheduling."

"Wow. I didn't know it would be this complicated."

"Really it isn't. We just have to get a schedule for you. Just keep in mind no Sundays. I am always off on Sundays."

"Oh. That's the best day for me," she said.

"Well, my apologies. I have to have at least one day off."

"It's okay. I just have to figure out how I can get time with my baby, you know?"

"You're a mom?"

"Yeah, I have a three-month-old little girl."

"That's cool. What's her name?"

"Deja."

"Awesome. I bet your husband is proud."

"Yeah, he's a proud daddy."

"How about you figure out a convenient time for you and your husband to set up an appointment and let me know? Then I'll see what schedule I can get you guys on."

"To be completely honest with you, Rayshon, like I said before, Devon will not be coming with me."

"Okay," he said. "Just let me know when you are ready."

"What about Tuesday? Can I meet with you on Tuesday morning? My assistant usually opens on Tuesdays. I can come around eight o'clock in the morning to pick out some type of schedule I can do."

"Tuesday is good, but unfortunately eight is bad because I have an eight o'clock that day. Seven is early, but I'm free from seven 'til eight after six o'clock. If not, I can't see you 'til two that afternoon."

"I guess I can come at seven, because Renee needs to leave by two thirty on Tuesdays, and I need to be at my store."

"Okay, seven it is," he said, and they hung up.

Ray was happy that she had finally called. He was even happier that he didn't have to look at her husband's face. He wondered what was going on with her marriage and why her man wouldn't be interested in working out with his wife. He went back to the football game he had been watching before she called, but he could hardly concentrate. He was now thinking about Leila, although he tried hard not to.

He picked up his phone, looked at the caller ID, and saved her number, so if something happened and she didn't show up, he'd be able to call her. He went into the kitchen to make a snack, and someone tapped on his door. He went to the door and saw that it was Trisha, a woman he absolutely didn't want to be bothered with.

One of his friends had hooked him up with her, but it was whack. Her head was not on straight. He tried to be nice, but she just wasn't getting the picture. He reluctantly opened the door, planning on talking to her at the door and not inviting her in.

"Hey, Trisha, what's up?" he asked, standing in front of the door.

"We gotta talk."

"Okay," he said, not inviting her in.

"Can I come in?" she asked.

He paused for a second and then stepped aside to let her in. His momma taught him better than that. "Look, I only got a few minutes because I have to head out soon," he said, lying to her. He didn't want to be bothered with this chick. She was cute and all, but she had no ambitions, and she had that "I'm waiting on a rich man to marry and take care of me" mentality. Ray's mom was a strong single mother, and if she didn't teach him anything else, she had always instilled in him, "God bless the child that's got his own."

"What's going on?" he asked her after she took a seat.

"I didn't wanna stop by unannounced, but you haven't returned any of my calls."

"Business is booming, and I've been mad busy," he said, making an excuse. He was busy, yes, but not too busy to return a phone call.

"We have a problem," she said.

He looked at her, confused. What type of problem could they possibly have? "We have a problem?" he asked.

"Yes, we do."

"Okay. Are you gon' tell me what this problem is?"

"Yeah, but can I have a drink of water?"

"Sure."

He went into the kitchen and got her a bottle of water from the fridge. He handed it to her, and she opened it and drank almost the entire bottle. Ray sat there, waiting for her to get to why she was there. She finished her water and sat there for a few moments, not saying anything.

"Hey, Trisha," he said.

She jumped like he had snapped her out of a trance. "Oh, yeah," she said.

This chick is nuts.

"I don't want you to be mad," she said.

"Stop beating around the bush. Come on, Trish, spit it out."

"I'm pregnant," she said.

He didn't react. "How is that my problem?"

"Because you're the father," she said.

He couldn't believe she said it with a straight face. "Well, my dear, you may wanna check your calendar, because I'm not the one."

"Yes, you are."

"How do you figure?"

"Come on, Ray, I'm not lying."

"I know you would have liked for this to work, but it didn't, okay? You can take your show on the road, because you are not pregnant by me. Now I'm not gonna argue with you. I'm just gonna ask you to leave, and I'd like for you to not call me anymore."

"How you gon' act like you innocent? I wouldn't be here if I weren't absolutely positive it was yours."

"I can see you're a little loony. Or maybe you've been fucking around so much you don't keep track of who you mess with. It is more likely for me to find a million dollars on the street than to be your baby's daddy."

"You're such an asshole. I will see your coward ass in court!" she yelled.

Ray was insulted and pissed. "Listen, I didn't wanna go there, but you've forced me. I have to talk to you like the dumb ass you are being. Unless you can conceive in your jaws, that is not my baby. The night we made out, all we did was oral. Let me take that back. All you did was oral. You were so messed up, you did your thang, and I didn't even get to nut in you, or anywhere near you, because after three minutes of you damn near performing surgery on my man, I pulled you off. I calmed you down and left you in bed by yourself. The next morning when you got up, you assumed that we got it on, but we didn't. I haven't returned your calls because it was a totally jacked-up date. After you drank Long Island after Long Island, I was turned off.

"After I dropped you off the next day, I was hoping you remembered how you acted the night before and would be too embarrassed to call me, but when you called and called and called, I knew you weren't wrapped too tight." After he said it, he wished he could have taken back that last statement. "I'm sorry, but I am not the one."

She looked at him without saying anything, and he could see how foolish she must have felt. She put the water bottle down on the coffee table and got up and left.

Ray shook his head and laughed his ass off. He called his boy and told him what went down. He laughed himself to sleep that night.

Chapter Eight

When Leila got to Ray's building, she was nervous. She was ten minutes early, and she didn't want to wait in the truck. She got Deja out, walked into his building, and took the elevator to his floor. When she knocked, she heard his voice say, "Give me a minute." She stood and waited until he opened the door.

"Hey, Leila, come on in and have a seat over here. I'm still with a client, so give me a few minutes," he said. She followed him and had a seat. She was a few minutes early, so she didn't mind waiting.

He dashed back to the steps and ran up in a flash. Leila could hear them finishing up. When the session was over, they came down, and Leila saw a sexy woman. She was beautiful, Leila thought. She felt embarrassed. The woman had on a two-piece workout suit, and her stomach looked like she did a million sit-ups a day. Leila felt intimidated. Maybe it was a bad idea for her to be there.

"Hi, I'm Christa," the woman said when she noticed Leila.

"Hello, I'm Leila."

"I see you are here to get rid of those pounds from the baby."

Leila thought that was rude and not a nice thing to say. "I guess you can say that." She didn't know how to respond. She was a plus-size woman, and looking at Christa, she felt like the ugly, fat girl.

"You've come to the right place, because he is magical." She made Ray sound like a miracle worker. "In no time, you'll be in a two-piece," Christa said.

Leila wanted to slap her. It was obvious that Christa had never had a weight problem or a baby. "Yeah, I've heard," she said, hoping Christa would finish putting on her jacket and leave her alone.

"Good luck on your weight-loss journey. And, Ray, I will see you tomorrow," Christa said and finally made her exit.

Ray closed the door and turned his attention to Leila. "Good morning, Miss Leila. I'm glad to see you. This is your little one?" he asked. He turned the baby seat around to see Deja. She was awake and started laughing as soon as he started talking to her. "She is precious and beautiful, just like her momma," he said.

Leila blushed. "Thank you," she said, smiling.

"Yeah, I need to get down to business. Two beautiful women in my place is too much pressure," he said, and they laughed.

They went over the schedule, and Leila thought she'd start with Tuesdays and Thursdays. She chose eleven. That way, the baby would be at daycare, and Renee would be at the store. She was excited and anxious to get started. He told her to come twenty minutes early so they could go over nutrition and how to separate good carbs from bad carbs.

They chatted until his eight o'clock arrived. Leila wanted to kill herself when she saw the next diva he had to train. Ray was fine, yes, and the women coming in there had to be trying to get with him. As good as he looked and as fine as the two women Leila saw were, she felt like chopped liver. As good as they both looked, she knew they didn't have to work hard to get or keep a man.

She wondered how many of his clients he was dating or sleeping with. Christa did say he was good. *How good and good at what?* she wondered as he let her and Deja out. She waited for the elevator, wondering if she was really ready to come back. She didn't want to look like a fat fool in front of Ray, but it was too late. She had already signed her contract.

On Thursday, a couple days later, after Leila talked herself into actually showing up, she parked her Armada on his street. She had on sweats and an oversized T-shirt under her jacket. She looked at the underweight miniature woman coming down the hallway on her way to Ray's loft, and she wanted to turn back and go home. *Where are these flat-tummy, plump-ass youngsters coming from?* Leila wondered.

"Hello," the woman said as she passed.

"Hi, how are you?" Leila asked with a smile.

"I'm fine."

You got that right. She got to Ray's door and tapped a couple of times.

"Hey, Leila, good to see you," Ray said when he opened the door. He looked even sexier than he had before. He had on a black tank, and his shoulders looked good enough to eat.

"Hey. I hope I'm not too early," she said.

"No, you're fine. Come on in and let me get your folder." He walked over to his office area, pulled out a folder, and picked up blank forms that looked like a profile, but Leila wasn't sure. She was happy to see that his business was legit and he wasn't running some type of ghetto-fabulous establishment.

"Okay, before we get started today, I wanna tape you and get your weight."

"Huh? Is this standard?"

"Yes, my dear, I'm afraid it is. How else will we know if we are making progress?" he asked with a smile.

"I don't know. Maybe this was a bad idea."

"You don't have to feel embarrassed or uncomfortable with me. I've seen it all. Your weight and your size are fine. I know why you're here, so relax," he said. His tone was soothing, but she was still uncomfortable. "I'm here to help you get started on a workout regimen. That's it. After you have learned the tools to be healthier, you will no longer need me. So, come on, let me get your measurements so we can get started."

She was hesitant but stood up to allow him to tape her.

"You look terrified. Just relax."

"Please don't make me get on that scale," she begged.

"I'm sorry, but you have to."

"No, please, Ray. I really don't want to," she cried. She was already embarrassed at the numbers he wrote down for her measurements.

"Hey, I betcha I can tell you how much you weigh. If I'm wrong, you don't have to get on the scale today, but if I can guess within five pounds of what you weigh, you have to tell me."

"What?" she asked, confused.

"I'm going to turn my head. You get on the scale, and if the number on that scale is within five pounds of what I guessed, you have to tell me today. If I'm wrong, you don't have to tell me 'til you are ready to tell me."

"Okay, Mr. Johnson, what's your guess?" she asked, up for the challenge.

"Um, let me see. Step back a little. You are five feet five, so I'd say two seventeen."

She wondered why he said such a high number. She couldn't be over 200 pounds.

"Two seventeen? You know you're wrong," she said, shaking her head at him.

"Yep, I say two seventeen, and you, my dear, must have not weighed yourself in a while."

Now Leila was determined to prove a point. "Okay, mister, turn around," she said.

He did, and she stepped onto the scale. The digital numbers stopped on 221, and she almost hit the floor. For one, she couldn't believe that he was within five pounds, and for another, she didn't realize she weighed that much.

"Okay, okay. I guess you do know your stuff."

"Was I right?"

"No, it was two twenty-one," she said and sat down in the chair. She felt like crying.

"Hey, don't look so disappointed. You will be all right. You just have to be patient, and you will see changes," he said.

Leila knew he was trying to make her feel better, but she didn't. "That's easy for you to say. Now I feel like I have to stop eating for the rest of my life."

"No, that will only make it worse. Here is a list of things you can have a whole lot of and another list of the things I want you to stay away from," he said.

She looked over the page he handed her. "Rice? I can't eat rice?" she asked. She loved Chinese food.

"You can, but stay away from white rice. Brown rice is okay, but not much of it."

"And potatoes and sour cream? I feel like I'm going on punishment."

"Leila, come on. Some of these things are okay in moderation, but to jump-start your metabolism, you are going to have to make changes to your diet."

"Damn, why did I have to wait 'til thirty to gain weight? I've never had an issue with my weight. For years I maintained a ten, but now I can't even shop in the mall."

"Don't get discouraged before you try it. This is the beginning. It will take at least twenty-one days before your body and appetite will adjust to this, but you have to be here to give it one hundred and ten percent, or else you are wasting my time and your money."

"I know. I'm ready."

"That's what I wanted to hear. You can do this."

"Yeah, I know. It isn't gonna be easy, but I'm ready."

"Let's go up so we can get started," he said. She followed him up the steps. "Today we are gonna start with the basics. You will be a little sore tomorrow, but please don't let that stop you from coming back. It will get easier as your muscles get used to the change, so give it time."

"Okay," she said, listening carefully to everything he said.

"We're going to start with stretching. If anything hurts or if you can't do something, let me know," he said gently, making Leila feel more relaxed and comfortable.

The session felt kind of weird to her, but slowly she got more into it. When it was over, she was happy she decided to sign up. She also knew she was going to have to get her hair braided. The little they had done had her sweating like a pig.

Ray gave her a bottle of water and made sure she was feeling okay. She smiled and assured him that everything was cool.

He walked her to the door. "Was it fun?" he asked.

"Yes, it was. Hard, but fun for the most part."

"That's what I like to hear."

"And thanks so much for being so patient with me, because there were moments where I know I looked stupid," she said, and they laughed.

"You did fine. Just keep in mind that things don't happen overnight. You have to be patient and stick to it."

"I plan to."

"Good. Then I'll see you on Tuesday. Try to go by that diet plan over the weekend. Don't let this part be a waste," he said and smiled.

"I will. And thanks again."

"It was my pleasure," he said.

She walked away and smiled all the way to her truck. She wondered if he was always that pleasant and treated folks like he had treated her. That was completely opposite of what she expected from him. She had judged him and made him out to be an egotistical jerk, but he was far from it.

She wondered if he had a woman, then tried to stop herself from going there. He was fine, yes, but no way was she beautiful enough for him to want her. If Devon didn't want her, Rayshon, fine to the bone, wouldn't think twice about her.

Not when he had opportunities to be in contact with women like Christa and that woman she saw earlier in the hall.

She drove back to the bookstore with fantasies of Rayshon. She wished she looked like she looked when she was in college. You couldn't tell her she wasn't fine back then. She had the body and the brains, and she remembered how crazy Devon was about her. She glanced at herself in the mirror and wondered how any man would ever want her like that again, especially Rayshon. The only solution she could come up with as to why he treated her so kindly was that he wanted her check to clear.

He was pretty pricey, but if he could make her look like one of his other trainees, she'd give him a million bucks. She got back to the bookstore and tried to get him out of her mind, but spent the entire afternoon talking to Renee about him. She knew that she'd never have a man like him in this lifetime, but she enjoyed fantasizing about it.

Chapter Nine

Leila was getting into her truck when her cell phone rang. She looked at the screen and saw it was Devon. She got in and settled into her seat before she answered.

She answered and said, "Yes, Devon, I am on my way." She had to pick up the baby from him.

"Good, because we need to talk." He sounded melancholy.

"What is it? Is Deja okay?" she asked, concerned.

"DJ is fine. That isn't what I want to discuss with you, Lei."

"What is it? You sound so serious."

"I got the divorce papers today . . . yesterday," he said.

Butterflies fluttered in Leila's stomach. She knew he'd be getting them soon, but she wasn't ready to discuss it with him. "I will be there in about thirty minutes," she said and ended the phone call.

She smiled because she was relieved, but at the same time, she was a bit nervous about seeing him face-to-face. She rehearsed the speech that she had planned to say to him when the time came for her to follow through with her plan to finally give him what he'd threatened to give her for months.

When she got to his place, she parked in the guest parking stall and opened the visor to check herself in the mirror. She had gotten her hair done earlier that day, and she wanted to make sure she still looked good. She powdered her face and reapplied her lip gloss, then checked her teeth to make sure there was no food stuck in between them. Finally, she popped a mint into her mouth and cut the engine.

When she got to the door, she lifted her arm to knock, but Devon opened the door before she could. "Come on in," he said and walked away quickly. He went into the kitchen, and she figured he was cooking, because the room smelled heavenly.

She went over to her baby, who was in her playpen. "Hey, girlfriend. How ya doing, baby girl?" she asked, picking up her baby.

Deja was getting so big, and her mommy was getting so small. Well, at least dropping pounds at a rapid but healthy rate. She was looking good and was down thirty-five pounds since she started working with Ray, and it showed. She felt good.

"You are looking good," Devon said, coming up behind her.

"Thanks," she said and put the baby back down. She sat on the sofa and waited for Devon to get started with their discussion.

"How are things at the store?" he asked.

"Things are good. And at your company?" she asked, not really caring, just being courteous. Ever since Michelle had been a factor, and she worked at the same company, Leila made it a point not to bring up his job.

"Things are going really good."

"That's good to hear," she said. "What did you wanna talk about?" She didn't want to talk about the divorce, but she had to get this conversation on the road.

"Do you want a drink?" he asked.

She raised an eyebrow. "You know I'm still nursing."

"I didn't know if maybe you had some milk pumped. I didn't think. I can get you some water or juice," he offered.

"I'm fine. I can't stay too much longer. I have to go by the store and do the books."

"I guess I should get straight to the point, huh?"

"That would be a good idea."

"Lei, why are you doing this?" he asked her, looking pitiful.

"Come on, Devon. You've been telling me every other month that you want a divorce. Now that I finally give you what you said you wanted, you ask me why?"

"I changed my mind, okay? I love you and DJ, and I know I've made a huge mistake. I'm willing to drop everything right now if you just give me another chance. I don't want the divorce. I want you, and I want Deja. Please, I want to come home."

He looked genuine, but Leila wasn't buying it. She wasn't going to let him get back into her life to hurt her all over again. She had given him opportunity after opportunity to come home. Now her head was clear, and she was ready to let go. She had moved on, starting fresh.

"I can't go there with you. Why can't you just get this over with? You know you don't wanna be with me. You just don't want me to be with someone else. It is perfectly fine for you to be with Michelle, but I can't have the freedom to get on with my life?" She stood up.

"Is that why you are divorcing me, because of Michelle? You're going through with the divorce because you think I'm with Michelle?"

"No, Devon, I'm not jealous of that little lying trick. I couldn't care less about Michelle. I just want a life too. You have this fabulous single life where you have parties, dating, and who knows what, and all I've done is sit around and wonder if you'd come back to me. I'm tired of wondering if this will be the day or if it will be tomorrow or will you ever. I sat around for a long time, waiting and waiting."

"You don't have to wait on me. I'm right here, and I'm ready to start over now. I promise that I am ready to love you like you deserve to be loved. Like I should have been doing for the longest time. I know I messed up. I am not saying that I was the stand-up dude who always did right by you. But can't you just forgive me and let the past go?" he asked, pleading. He moved closer to her, and she backed away. She had to keep her distance because she wasn't completely over him.

"I have forgiven you," she said, moving across the room. "I don't hate you. I just can't trust you. When I was pregnant, you walked out on me. You left me alone. I cried so much and prayed that you'd come to your senses and come home. You abandoned me when I needed you the most because you were so disgusted that I changed. You criticized me and treated me like

I was this burden, and you looked at me
like I was a nobody." She tried not to cry while
her mind went back to the time when she was
alone and pregnant without her husband. How
he'd passed through like she was just his baby's
momma, with no regard to her feelings. "What's
so different now? Why do you want me now?"

"I've always wanted you. I've loved you since
the first day I met you. I just had a stupid moment. I went through this horrible, selfish phase,
and I know I treated you bad. I'm so sorry, baby.
Please? I don't want this divorce. I want you."
He walked over to her and put his arms around
her waist.

"Stop it. Please stop. Just stop it, okay?" She
walked away from his embrace.

"Come here, baby. Look at me, please. Come
on, look at me," he said, following her.

"No, Devon. I gotta go, okay? Get DJ's things. I
gotta go," she said, moving to get the baby. Deja
was laughing and playing, having a good time by
herself.

"I can't let you walk out. I don't want this.
I don't want this divorce. I won't give you a
divorce," he said, raising his voice.

Leila was touched. She wanted to turn to him
and say, "Okay," but she couldn't. She put the
baby back down and went into the bathroom

without saying another word to him. She shut the door and fought tears. She loved Devon, but she was over the heartache and drama. She wished he would have said something a long time ago. She wished he wanted their marriage back when she was pregnant, when she would have taken him back in a heartbeat.

Now things were so different, and as much as she hated their situation, it was what it was. She didn't want to be the bad guy like he was making her out to be. She had granted him his wish. For so many months, he had thrown the word "divorce" in her face. Time after time, she had asked him to come home and start over. Too many times, she begged him to come home and make their marriage work, but he had walked around doing his own thing. And now it was time for her to do the same.

She wiped her face and got herself together. She wasn't going to give in to him. She wasn't going to let him win. She was ready to end it, and he wasn't going to change her mind. She opened the door and went back into the living room. Devon was sitting on the sofa with the baby, and she stopped in her tracks at the sight of them together. Deja was laughing and making happy baby sounds as her daddy talked to her. Leila stood there and took it in for a moment, then jerked herself away from the thought of them being a happy family.

"You have her things? I gotta go," she said, picking up the baby's bottle from the playpen. Devon got up and handed Deja to Leila, and the baby started to cry.

"Aw, it's okay, baby girl. Mommy is ready to go," she said. Deja continued to cry for her daddy.

"Here, give her to me for a moment," he said, trying to take her out of Leila's arms.

"No, Devon. Please go and get her stuff. She'll be fine."

"I'm not going to let her cry like this," he said, still trying to get her out of Leila's arms.

"Okay. Here, take her," she said, giving in. She looked around. "Where is her bag?"

"In the bedroom," he said.

Leila went into his room to get her baby's things. His room was immaculately clean, and his big bed was made up so tight it looked like it had been professionally made. She took her focus off the bed and looked around for Deja's bag. She spotted it by the nightstand. Then she saw his cell phone. The light was flashing, and she couldn't resist picking it up. She touched the screen and saw six missed calls. All from Michelle.

She wondered how he was planning on getting back with her when Michelle was still in his life. She put the phone down and walked out. He was full of shit. He wanted to be a player when he still had something going on with Michelle, but she wasn't going to fall for that. She was in no mood to be crying over Devon again.

"Okay, Deja, we gotta go," she said. Again, Deja refused to go along with the program. She started to cut up again. "What is it, momma? Why are you being a bad girl?" Leila asked.

"Because she doesn't want to leave her daddy, that's what's wrong. She wants to stay."

"Well, I have stuff to do," she said impatiently.

"Look, she can stay here. You go do what you gotta do."

"Then what, come all the way back over here?"

"Call me when you are on your way home, and I'll bring her."

"No, Devon, that is too much. I can take her now. She is just gonna have to behave," Leila said, putting her foot down.

"I'm not doing anything tonight, and I don't mind keeping my angel. So go, and I'll bring her home."

"Are you sure?"

"Yes, I'm sure."

"Okay," she said and kissed her baby. "Mommy will see you later, sweetie pie," she said and grabbed her purse.

Devon looked like he was waiting for a kiss too. "I'll see you later, and we'll continue where we left off," he said.

"There is nothing more to discuss," she said, putting on her coat.

"Oh, there is," he said.

Leila opened the door to leave. "Whatever. I'll see you and Deja later," she said and shut the door.

Chapter Ten

"When are you gonna tell her?" Mario asked Ray.

"Tell who what?"

"Come on now, Ray. You have been my boy since forever, and I know that you are digging her."

"Man, you don't know what you are talking about. For one, that woman is married. For two, she is a client. And three . . . well, there's no three, but I'm not feeling her."

"Damn. Why do you always act like you are this cool cat, so laidback and not into these females? You act like it's impossible for you to dig a woman who is one of your so-called clients. Personally, I never figured it to be Leila. I always thought you'd be trying to get with one of them model chicks, but I see that you do like the heavy ones," he said and laughed.

"Hey, watch your mouth. You know I don't talk about people that way. We all can't be the same size and shape, and you know I don't dog people like that."

"Man, you act like you don't look at overweight women, or even men, and think that they look disgusting," Mario said, laughing again.

"No, I don't, because I am educated enough to know that obesity is a disease, you ass. If I wanted to make fun of overweight people or treat them like outcasts, I would have never gone into this line of business, dumb ass."

"Chill out. I'm just talking shit. The point is, you need to be honest and tell that woman you are feeling her. I can tell because you go to the bookstore more times than you go to the bathroom," he said, and they laughed.

"Man, g'on with that," Ray said, pushing Mario's shoulder.

"I'm serious, dude," Mario said. "You talk about her all the damn time."

"I don't. You bring her up more than I do. You must want her."

"Dawg, please. You know I don't bring that woman up. I don't know her like that, but every time we get together, all you do is find a way to bring her up. You be like, 'Man, Leila put me on to this book,' or, 'Man, Leila told me about this,' or, 'In our last session, Leila told me such-and-such.' If you can't be honest with her, at least tell me the truth. You are digging her, aren't you?"

Ray paused. He hesitated and decided to stick to his story. "She is a client. I don't mix business with pleasure."

"Yeah. That's why yo' ass is celibate now, because you only do business and no pleasure."

"You know I have a social life. I mean, not all my time is business. I'm out with you tonight, aren't I?" he asked and took a sip of his Hennessy.

"Yes, but that's because I wasn't gonna take no for an answer this time. I mean, since you and Katrina broke up, you're different."

"See, there you go. Why must you go there? When I am not thinking about that woman and my mind is completely rested, you go there." Ray took a gulp of his drink. Just thinking of his ex made him shake his head. "Can I get another one?" he asked the bartender.

"My bad. I was only saying, dude, you haven't had a woman in what, five or six years? When did y'all break up, again? '03? '02?"

Ray didn't find his friend amusing at all. "Look, it was '02, and I've had women since then." He paid the bartender after he put his drink down in front of him.

"Yes, you have had some ass, but a woman? Name one woman you went out with for more than a month since Katrina," Mario said.

Ray said nothing. No one came to mind.

"See, now what? I told you." Mario took a swallow of his beer.

"Ramona," Ray said suddenly. "Ha. Ramona, man." He smirked and took a sip of his drink.

"Oh, yeah, Ramona. Y'all kicked it for what, three months? Wow, that was deep."

"Damn, man, why you sweatin' me?"

"Because I think you'd be a happier man if you'd be honest and tell that woman that you like her. I mean, what's the worst that can happen?"

"She could ruin my business. I could regret it for the rest of my life. Let's see, Mario. How about me losing a client? She is doing so well, and if I go messing with our professional relationship, she may fall back into that rut."

"What rut?"

"Look, she and her husband had some issues, okay? And she was hurt by him. I don't want to get involved with her and things don't work. I mean, Leila is a very unique lady. She is smart and vibrant. She has come out of the shell she was in, and her confidence is higher than it was the day I met her at her bookstore," he said, taking another sip.

"What you are saying is you are not gonna get involved with this woman because you're afraid you will hurt her?"

"No, I won't hurt her," he said defensively.

"So, what is your problem?" Mario asked. "I mean, it is obvious that you dig this woman. And from what you've told me in our hundreds of conversations, she is now divorcing him and has decided to move on with her life. The ex is not a factor. What are you, my friend, afraid of?"

Ray was quiet for a moment. "I'm not afraid, okay? I just think it's not the right time to pursue Leila."

"Then when do you think it will be the right time? After she goes off and meets some other dude? Yes, she is a thick sista, but she is also a beautiful sista, and you sitting up here, chilling and backing up. One day she is gonna come to one of them little sessions and tell you about some guy named Dexter St. Cock, and you gon' wish you had stepped up to the plate."

That made Ray think for a moment. What if Mario was right? Yes, Leila was very pretty, and any man with eyes would be foolish to look past her. Suddenly, he wasn't in the mood to be at their spot anymore. He paid for another drink and told Mario that after he finished, he would be heading out.

He got up and went to the bathroom, and when he came back, there were two fine sistas sitting at the bar near his stool. He hesitated to approach because he saw that Mario had already engaged in conversation with them.

He took his seat, said hello, and exchanged introductions with them. He was set to leave, but Mario practically begged him to stay for another round, and he agreed. After a little conversation, he found out that Karen, the one sitting close to him, was in nursing school and worked at a nearby hospital as an intern. He couldn't make out too much of what her friend was saying because of the music, but he nodded and was attentive to the conversation.

Karen was pretty, with a vanilla skin tone and wavy hair that hung a little past her shoulders. Although she was sitting, Ray determined she was about five feet tall and about 130 pounds. Her friend, Leslie, also fair complexioned, was about five foot seven and about 150 pounds. They were both very attractive.

Karen flirted with Ray, but his mind was not there. It was on Leila. He wondered what she was doing and where she was. Could she be out on a date with another man? Could she be in another man's arms? He tried to focus on the conversation with Karen, but it was difficult for him to do.

"You're a personal trainer?" Karen asked.

"Yes, that's what I do," he responded with a fake smile. He didn't want to be rude to her, and since her friend had found her way to the stool on the other side of Mario, he felt obligated to talk to her.

"You think you can whip my body into shape?" she asked, flirting heavily. He knew he had to end the conversation quickly before she asked him about setting up an appointment.

"It looks like you have that under control," he said, giving her a quick once-over. She didn't need his services.

"I do what I can, but I know with a little training I could always look better," she said, giving him a sexy smile.

"There is always room for improvement." He looked away. He just couldn't take his mind off what Mario had said about Leila getting with another dude.

"Yes, there is. So do you think I can get a session?" She leaned over, giving him a peep at her cleavage.

"I'd have to see about getting you on my books," he said and sipped his drink. He tried to move his eyes from her cleavage, but it was difficult because she had on a low-cut top that exposed her perfectly round mounds, and they looked good.

"How about you do that?" She smiled.

"Oh yes, I will," he said, trying to make her feel like a sexy woman. She was attractive, and Ray made it a habit to always make a woman feel like a woman. And she was a woman who had it going on. "Listen, I gotta run. I have another spot that I promised my sister I would hit, and if I don't show, you know how that goes," he said, lying.

"So soon?" she asked, looking disappointed.

"Yeah. It's like her man's birthday or some shit, and I promised I'd be there." He hated to lie, but he had to bounce. "Here is my card. You can call me to set up that appointment," he said, handing it to her. He stood up and put on his leather jacket.

"Ray, man, you out?" Mario asked.

"Yeah, man. You know I got to go by Rhonda's. It's Kenny's birthday," he said, acting like he had mentioned it earlier.

"Oh, yeah, man, I almost forgot," he said, going along with Ray. "Excuse me, Leslie, I'm gonna walk my boy out."

"Okay, I'll be right here waiting," she said, giving him a sexy smile.

Mario turned and walked Ray out the door.

"Thanks for not busting a brother out," Ray said when they got outside.

"No problem. I know what's up."

"Well, you, my friend, don't go getting into any trouble. Last I heard, you and your woman were on the road to success."

"I know. I'm gonna talk a little shit and hang out, and I am gonna be out shortly. Trust," he said, and they shook.

"You betta," Ray said, "because your woman will have your ass on the six o'clock news."

"True, true. Get home safe."

"You too, dawg," Ray said and headed toward his Tahoe.

"Yo," Mario yelled out to him.

"What's up?"

"Talk to the woman. Be real," Mario said.

"Soon, man, soon," Ray responded and walked away.

It was still early when he got home, not even eleven o'clock. He decided to get on the treadmill to think. After running two miles, it still wasn't even midnight, so he showered and put on some sweats. He walked over at his work area and turned on the light. He looked through his file cabinet and took out Leila's file. He opened it and looked at the picture he had taken the day she'd started, and he smiled. There was already a difference in the way she looked.

Not that he didn't like her before or he didn't find her attractive then. He was just proud of her success. She was doing what she was supposed to do, and it showed. He put her file away and looked over at the clock. Eleven forty. It would be rude to call her that late at night. He turned out the light on his desk and went into the living room and turned on the television. After an hour of nothing, he decided to turn in.

He got in bed, and as soon as he shut his eyes, his cell phone rang. He looked at the clock. It was a quarter 'til one. He thought it might be Mario, but when he looked at the caller ID, he didn't recognize the number.

"Hello," he said in his deep and sexy tone.

"Hey, are you still out?" the voice on the other end asked.

"Who is this?" he asked, sitting up in his bed.

"This is Karen. I was calling to see if you were able to fit me in your schedule."

He knew what time it was. "When are you available?" he asked, going along with her. It was damn near one o'clock in the morning, and he was still a man, and she was fine.

"I can be available in about thirty minutes. Where are you located?" she asked.

"I see you are ready to burn some calories?"

"Oh, yes I am. How about you?"

"I could use a good workout before I go to sleep," he said, standing and moving over to his nightstand. He opened it to check his supply of condoms. He was good.

He told her that the address was on the business card he had given her, then hung up. He went into the bathroom and brushed his teeth again, then turned on some soft music and waited for her to get to his place. He lit a few candles to set the mood, and before he could make a mental note not to think about Leila, there was a knock on the door.

He opened the door, and Karen stood in the doorway. He invited her in and took her coat. They didn't talk much before he had her in his bed. She was a wildcat in bed, and he enjoyed the night they shared together. He fell right to sleep and dreamed of him and Leila. He dreamed of her being with him in his kitchen, cooking a meal, drinking wine, and laughing with each other. He dreamed of touching her face and caressing her cheek. He was happy in his dream, just enjoying her smiles and hearing her laughter.

The next morning, when he woke up next to Karen, he remembered the exciting night he had shared with her. She was cool, and he enjoyed her, but she wasn't Leila. He didn't wake her when he eased out of bed to go to the bathroom. He went into the kitchen, poured himself a glass of orange juice, and opened the door to retrieve his Sunday paper. He glanced at the clock and saw it was only eight.

He sat at the island in his kitchen and read the paper and enjoyed his juice. After an hour, he went back into his bedroom. Karen was still asleep. He was a gentleman and didn't wake her. He went back out and pulled the door closed behind him before pulling all the curtains in his loft open to expose the downtown Chicago view. It was glorious. He turned on the music and proceeded to do some cleaning like he always did on Sundays.

His place was never a mess, but he made it a point to keep the dust in check and keep it spotless. It was not only his home, but it was where he did business. After he dusted and swept, he organized the office area. By the time he was done, it was after eleven, and Karen hadn't budged. He didn't want to be an asshole, but she had to go. He had to get water and energy bars to stock up for the week, and he wasn't in the habit of leaving strange women at his place.

He went into the bedroom. "Hey, Karen, wake up," he whispered in her ear.

She grunted and wiped her eyes. "What time is it?"

"Eleven thirty," he said.

She sat up in bed. "Damn, I'm sorry. I don't know why I slept so late," she said, getting up and looking around for her belongings. He had put her things on the chair neatly.

"It's cool. There is a toothbrush and fresh towels in the bathroom for you," he said, opening the drapes in his room, exposing yet another beautiful view.

She stood up, and he admired her perfect, petite body. She had no stretch marks, and her breasts were still standing tall. He watched as she walked to the bathroom without grabbing anything to cover up with. Karen was certainly not shy.

"Thank you," she yelled from the bathroom.

"No problem," he said and went back into the living room.

"This is a nice place," she said, coming out of the bedroom completely dressed a few minutes later.

"Thank you," he said, placing a glass of orange juice and a bagel on the island for her. He removed the frying pan from the stovetop and put her eggs on the plate with the bagel and gave her a little bowl of fresh fruit.

"Wow, you didn't have to do this, Ray," she said, sitting in front of the plate.

"It's no hassle. My momma always told me, 'If you have someone over, always make them feel welcome.'"

"Your momma did a good job raising you with manners. Men are usually cold after a night of sex. Have your clothes on the porch the next morning," she said and chuckled.

"Well, my dear, maybe you should choose your sex partners a little more carefully," he said and put the pan in the sink.

"I'm working on that," she hissed.

If her tone were a razor, I wouldn't have a dick left. "I'm sorry. That was a joke. I didn't mean that to offend you," he said. He wasn't trying to be rude or disrespectful.

"It's cool. I'm okay," she said. She ate her food, and when she was finished, he took her plate and placed it in the sink. "What's up there?" she asked, pointing to the gym area.

"That's where I do my sessions."

"Can I see?" she asked.

"Sure," he said and took her up.

"What's your story, Mr. Ray? Are you single?"

"Yep."

"Why is that?" she asked, sitting on the workbench.

"Because I work a lot and I make it my business not to date my clients. Since most of the women I come in contact with are clients, that leaves little room for romance."

"Well, since you live by that rule, I don't want to become a client." She moved closer to him.

"You don't want to enhance this body?" he asked, grabbing her ass.

"I'd rather burn calories with you the way we did last night," she said and kissed him.

"That's not a bad idea," he said and removed her shirt.

The next thing he knew, his mouth was sucking on one of her nipples. She stroked his man, and he caressed her back. He picked her up, and she wrapped her legs around his waist and kissed him again. He remembered his condoms were downstairs, so he carried her down the steps and took her into his bedroom.

After they went at it again, they kissed each other goodbye, and Ray told her he'd call her. He showered and dressed to go out to do his errands. When he got back to his loft, he changed his sheets and finished cleaning his bedroom and bathroom. He sat on the sofa to read a book that he had gotten from the bookstore a few days ago, and thoughts of Leila returned to his mind. He finished out his day without calling Karen. His focus had gone back to the woman he wanted, and it was not her.

Chapter Eleven

Leila avoided Devon all weekend. When he brought Deja home Sunday, he tried to stick around to talk, but she pretended she was on her way out when he got there. She told him she would call him when she got home, but she never did. All that evening, he called and called, and she refused to answer. He showed up at the bookstore the next day, and she told him that she just needed time to think. He finally accepted that answer and cut her some slack. She was confused and unsure of what to do next. She cared for him, but she didn't trust him.

She wondered how long it would last if she let him back home. Would she have to worry about him messing around with that five-pound, twelve-ounces little trick named Michelle? If she gained any of her weight back, would he trip out again and dog her? If she got pregnant again, would he pull another disappearing act? She thought about all these things. Why did she have to go through this? Why couldn't he just sign the papers and call it a day?

She rode to Ray's loft with heavy thoughts. She thought about canceling her appointment, but she didn't want to break her routine. The way she was feeling, she knew that if she canceled, it would lead to ice cream and cookies on the couch. She had come too far to still allow Devon to control her life. She was finally conquering things on her own and in her own way. She was determined not to let the situation with the divorce set her back.

When she got to Ray's, she got off the elevator. Coming down the hall was the one and only Christa. She looked good, as she always did, but Leila was in no mood for her smart-ass mouth.

"Leila, how nice to see you," she said with her fake smile.

"Nice to see you," Leila returned.

"Ooh, girl, you might have to give him a minute because he worked me over real good today," she purred, sounding like a desperate tramp.

"I'm sure Ray will be all right. He has a way of doing the same for all of us," Leila snapped. She wanted her to know she was no more special to Ray than she was. Just like Christa got her money's worth, so did she.

"I see. Well, you enjoy. Too bad he sees you after he sees me," Christa said, walking to the elevator.

"Actually, it's a good thing. All you do is get him warmed up for me. Enjoy your day, hon."

Christa glared at her, stormed down the hall, and jabbed the elevator button repeatedly. Leila knew she was annoyed that Ray might like her just as much as he did her. No skinny chick wanted to feel threatened by a fat chick. Leila chuckled.

She tapped on the door and heard Ray tell her to come on in, so she pushed the door open. He wasn't in the living room. She took off her coat and put it on the coatrack by the door and went upstairs. She was used to coming and knowing what to do to get started. She stretched and wondered what was keeping him. She got onto the treadmill and started her twenty-minute warm-up. When he finally came up, she was already ten minutes into her walk.

Ray barely looked at her, and she wondered what was bothering him. He apologized for keeping her waiting. When she was done, she looked at him. He looked good. His haircut looked like it was just done, and he smelled wonderful. He didn't look as if he had just had a session with Christa, and when he spoke, she could smell the freshness of his breath. Not that he stank before, but he was extra fresh, what some would call "funky fresh."

Normally they laughed and talked during their session, but that day was different. Ray was kind of quiet, and she didn't know why. She was normally a chatterbox, but her issues with Devon had her at a loss for words herself, so things were oddly strange. When the session was over, instead of her hanging around chatting with him like usual, she left.

She drove back to the store, wondering if something did finally go down with him and Christa. *Maybe that's what was keeping him. He had to shower and freshen up so I wouldn't smell sex on him.* She didn't know why, but it made her jealous. "That skinny bitch," she said out loud to herself as she drove away. "Monique is right, they are evil," she said. "First Michelle, now Christa. They think they can just have all the men."

When she got back to the store, things were a bit busy. Leila didn't hesitate to help Renee take care of the customers. After the crowd was cleared, Leila took her things into the back. She looked up and saw Renee standing in the doorway.

"What?" Leila asked.

She stepped into the office. "You gon' take him back, aren't you?" she asked, sounding disappointed.

"I don't know." Leila took off her snow boots and put on her comfy shoes.

"Don't let him trick you. You've come so far." Renee's voice was full of concern.

"That's easy for you to say. You have a man," Leila snapped.

Renee's hand flew to her chest, and her mouth dropped open. "Excuse me?" she said.

"Yes, Renee, I said it. You have a man. You walk around here, and you keep trying to convince me I shouldn't give my husband another chance when you go home to your husband every damn night. Look at me. I'm not a size six like you. Men are not beating down my door. It is so easy for you. You simply walk down the street and guys are trying to get with you. When you and I are together, guys treat me like I'm invisible. I have one man who is really trying to be with me. I don't know if I will ever have a man even half as fine as Devon approach me, and you keep trying to tell me to just forget him and let him go. News flash, I am lonely, and I am horny as hell. You might not understand it, but as much as Devon has done me wrong, I feel like taking him back so I can have someone to want me again."

Renee nodded. "I'm your friend, and I am not looking down on you. I know what damage Devon has done. I have been here with you since the day he walked out, and I have watched you suffer and cry so many times over him. I want what you want for you. I want whatever you decide suits you best, and if that is with Devon, so be it. But I see a new woman. You are beautiful, Lei, and if a man can't see that, then he has the problem.

"Don't settle for Devon for the sake of not being alone, because if he hurts you or does what he did again, you are going to hate yourself for allowing him to come back. That is not what I want for you. You are my friend, and I love you. You deserve to be happy. The right man will come along, and you won't be lonely. You deserve a good man in your life. And be honest, do you really want Devon back?"

"You don't understand. There's more to it than that. We have a child—"

Renee stopped her. "No, Lei, no. That's not what I asked you. Do you want Devon back?" she asked again.

Tears began to fall from Leila's eyes. She couldn't answer that and be honest with her friend. "I don't know right now. I just don't know," she said, not saying no. She didn't really want Devon back, but she didn't want to have to eat her words if they got back together.

"Take your time. I promise that, whatever you decide, I will support you, and I will always be here for you." Renee walked over to Leila and hugged her.

The bell on the front door chimed. Renee went out to take care of the customer, and she gave Leila a few moments to be alone.

After they closed, Leila went down the street to pick up Deja. Devon's car was parked out front. *Oh, Lord.* When she got inside, he was signing Deja out.

"You didn't tell me you were coming to pick the baby up today," she said. "You know the rules."

"I know, I know. I was going to wait here for you. I didn't know if you had picked her up yet. I thought I'd take my two girls out to dinner."

"Aw, I'm so tired."

"Come on. Come to dinner with me," he begged.

"Okay, Devon, okay," she said, not putting up a fight. If she did, he'd just hound her until she caved. And she was hungry anyway.

She followed him and the baby to a nearby restaurant. They ordered and ate, and Leila enjoyed being out with Devon. They hadn't been out in so long that it seemed strange. Before dinner was done, Deja was asleep in her seat. They finished and paid, and Devon offered to follow them home. Things were going well, so Leila didn't refuse. When they got home, he helped her and the baby inside, and he stayed until after Leila put her down for the night.

He hung around while she showered, and when she came down the stairs, she saw that he had dozed off on the sofa. She leaned over to wake him. When she touched him, he grabbed her arm.

"Oh, Lei, I'm sorry."

"It's okay. Um, it's getting late. You should go."

"Can I stay?" he asked.

"Not yet. I'm not ready," she said.

He rose up and kissed her. Her body went limp in his arms, and her nipples hardened. She told herself to resist him, but she couldn't. She wanted him. She wanted to be loved and touched. She wanted him to do her body the way he used to. They lay on the sofa, making out, and she moaned and panted from his kisses and his touch.

"I want you, Lei," he whispered as he sucked on her neck and licked her breast. Even though she was still full of milk, he sucked one into his mouth. She was so turned on that she felt the wetness between her legs. She wanted her husband.

"Let's go upstairs," she whispered.

"Okay," he said and stood. He took his phone and keys out of his pockets and put them on the coffee table. "Go on up, and let me lock up and set the alarm," he suggested.

Leila went upstairs, undressed, and got into bed. Lying there and waiting for him, she wondered if she was doing the right thing. Her body was on ten, and she couldn't think rationally. Finally, she decided she wanted him in her bed, so she stopped trying to figure it out.

It took Devon a few minutes, and she figured he had stopped to look in on Deja one more time before coming into her bedroom. When he came in, he undressed and climbed under the covers with her. It didn't take long for them to pick up where they had left off.

"You are so beautiful," he whispered.

Leila was touched. She hadn't heard that from him in years. She relaxed and let him take her body back to places she never thought she'd go with him again. Just when he was about to enter her, she stopped him.

"Wait, Devon, wait," she whispered. "You need this," she said, reaching over to get the condom she had taken out of the drawer when she'd gotten upstairs.

He looked shocked. "Are you serious?" he asked.

"As a heart attack," she replied.

He sighed but put it on, and then he slid inside.

She released a deep breath and moaned. She was happy to have him there. He filled her love nest with the divine strokes of his manhood, and she gave herself to him over and over again that night and one more time the next morning before they parted.

Leila had no idea where they were going or how they were going to end up. All she knew was that the night before had been magical. If their marriage could come back and be that strong, she was willing to try.

Chapter Twelve

Rayshon was ready. He wasn't going to let Leila leave without telling her how he felt or at least asking her out. He was willing to let her go as a client, and he had a highly recommended associate he would refer her to if she was willing to go out with him. He was mad at himself for not saying what he wanted to say to her the other day. He had chickened out, but he was not going to back down this time. He had practiced what he would say and had the words memorized.

Five minutes before her appointment, he was so nervous he took a shot of scotch to try to calm himself. He sat watching the clock, waiting for her to get there. Finally, there was a knock. He opened it the door, and Karen was there. He absolutely hadn't expected to see her.

"Karen, hey. What are you doing here?" he stammered.

"I was visiting a patient nearby, and I thought I'd stop by. I called you a few times, but I hadn't heard from you. I really wanted to see you, so here I am."

"Wow. Unfortunately, this is a bad time. I have a client on the way." Over Karen's shoulder, he saw Leila get off the elevator and make her way down the hall. He wished he could hit a button and make Karen's ass fall through a trap door.

Leila was at the door within seconds. "Hello," she said, giving Karen a bright smile.

Karen smiled back at her. "Hi, I'm Karen," she said.

"Hi, I'm Leila. Nice to meet you." Leila looked from Karen to Ray.

"Hey, Leila, go on in. This will only take a sec," he said, said stepping aside so she could pass. He pulled the door closed behind him and addressed Karen. "Listen, you are a sweet woman, and I had fun hanging out with you, but you cannot drop by my place whenever you feel like it. It's rude to drop by someone's home unannounced."

"And I feel that it's rude to tell a woman, 'I will call you' and never call. And I also think it's rude to not return a person's phone calls," she said, raising her voice.

"Shhhh," he said. "You are absolutely right. It was rude and inconsiderate. But I conduct my business here as well. So please don't come here making scenes and acting out. I'll talk to you later, but please, with all due respect, don't come to my home ever again without calling. I have a client waiting for me, and I have to work. I will call you soon, and we can talk, okay?" he said.

"Okay. And I am sorry for just dropping by your place. It will never happen again."

Ray was relieved that she didn't make a scene. "No problem," he said calmly, and he kissed the back of her hand.

He stood and watched until she got into the elevator, then went inside. Leila was already upstairs stretching.

"Hey, thanks for waiting," he said.

"No problem. I see you were in the middle of something."

"Yeah, but it's all good," he said, ready to get started. He was happy to see Leila. She looked radiant, he thought, and he tried not to stare.

"Was that your girlfriend?" she asked.

"Who?" he asked, surprised.

"Karen," she said, coming up on a sit-up.

"No. Why would you think that?"

"Because I haven't seen her before, and I know how you don't date clients."

"Well, my dear, Karen is not my girlfriend."

"I will say she is pretty and different from all the others."

"What do you mean, different?"

"She seems humble, not territorial. Most of them model-looking chicks I pass in the hall or run into coming out of here just stare like I'm a threat to them. Especially Christa. I am nowhere near as beautiful as she is, but she always acts like you're her man and I'm gon' take you. If I looked like her, I wouldn't let any other woman intimidate me."

"She ain't all that," Ray said.

Leila paused in the middle of another sit-up. "Have you not noticed her stomach? No matter how many sit-ups you make me do a month, my stomach will never look like that."

"So? You just had a baby," he said, not liking to hear her putting herself down.

"My baby is eight months old now, and my breasts, even after I'm done nursing, will never be that perky. What man is gonna look at me and want me over a woman like Christa?"

Ray bit his tongue to keep from saying that he would. "Listen, Leila," he said, nudging her back down to continue the workout, "beauty is only skin deep. Not all men look at women like Christa and just want them. Tons of men out there would want you over Christa," he said. *Like me.*

"Well, I wish I knew what planet they lived on because I would move there in a New York minute," she said. Ray stood up and walked away. "What? What's wrong? What did I say?" she asked.

"Okay," he said and clapped his hands. "I can't do this anymore."

"Do what?" Leila stood up. "What's going on? Did I do something?" she asked.

"No, no. You didn't do anything," he said, moving closer to her. "I tried to deny it and tried so hard to let it go, but I would, Leila. I would choose you over Christa any day. You are so beautiful to me, and I would do anything if you'd go out with me." There. He had finally told her. He held his breath.

"Are you serious? I thought you said that you don't get involved with your clients."

"I don't, and I promise you I've never done anything like this in my life. But I cannot stop thinking about you. You are perfect in my eyes, and I wouldn't change one thing about you. You make me laugh, and I can't seem to get your pretty smile out of my head," he said.

Leila's mouth opened. At first, nothing came out, and then she said, "Me? I can't believe what I'm hearing. I never actually thought of us ever being anything other than client and trainer, but right now, at this moment, I realize why I've been so jealous of Christa. It's because all along I thought you were sleeping with her. I mean. I'm just ordinary and fat. You are like Boris Kodjoe fine."

He chuckled. "That's cute. And you are Jill Scott fine to me," he said and kissed her.

It felt so good to finally taste her lips and hold her close. She reached up and put her arms around his neck, and they kissed deeply and passionately. Ray slowed the kiss and reached for her hands. He kissed her fingers and realized she had her wedding ring on.

A look of panic crossed Leila's face. "I didn't expect this, Rayshon."

"What's up? Are you and Devon working it out? Are y'all back together?"

"No. Well, I mean, I don't know. I've got to be honest with you. I was with him the last couple of nights, and things felt so right and so good. I was really considering it, but I haven't made a decision yet."

He backed up. "Do you love him?"

"Yes, I love him, but it's not the same."

"What do you mean? Either you love him or you don't." He felt like a fool. He wished he had kept his mouth shut and not shared his feelings with her.

"I love him, but our marriage has been over for a while. You and I have talked about this so many times, and you know how I feel. I went and filed my divorce, and ever since Devon got the papers, he has been trying to get me back. The last couple of nights I was with him, it just reminded me of how things used to be with us. I thought that maybe we had a chance."

"That's your answer right there," he said, angry. "I'm sorry for kissing you. I knew it was a mistake in the first place."

"What? Who do you think you are?" She put a hand on one hip. "You tell me a minute ago that you care about me and you can't stop thinking of me, then you kiss me like you just did, and now it was a mistake?"

"Yes, it was a mistake. I opened myself up to a woman who I thought was done with her past, done with her ex, but I find out that you are still with him. Yes, I made a mistake. I wasn't trying to kiss another man's wife. You told me weeks ago that you filed for the divorce, and I understood things to be over and done. It isn't, so kissing you was a mistake." He knew it wasn't right, but he couldn't help but still want her.

"It is over. In my heart, I know that it is over. Just the other day, my friend asked me if I wanted him, and I was too much of a coward to say no. But the truth is, no, I don't love him like that anymore. I honestly don't want him like that. I was just in love with the idea of us being a family again. I guess I was caught up in the fact that he was chasing me for a change, and I wasn't chasing him. I wanted to be loved and wanted, and he started to give me what I've wanted from him for so long.

"Even if you and I are never together, I can honestly say out loud that I don't want Devon. I just wanted the attention he gave me." Tears ran down her cheeks. "I never shut him down, because I didn't want him to stop his pursuit. I know it's silly, but I enjoyed him trying to date me again. To kiss me and touch me again. He treated me so horribly, and I begged him, Ray. Now, watching him beg gave me, I don't know, a sense of power."

"Can you allow me to do those things for you?" he asked, wiping her tears. "I can make you feel like a woman if you let me." He kissed her cheek then her lips.

She let go.

Leila's body came alive, and she found herself giving in to Ray like a horny teenager in the back seat of a car. She didn't ask any questions or say anything at all when he led her downstairs into his bedroom. Despite what she told him earlier she'd had thoughts of him in the past but always shrugged them off because she didn't think she was a woman he'd be interested in. She used to think he was full of shit when he used to compliment her and flirt with her, but as he licked her body, she realized he was a grown-ass man, and he wasn't playing any games.

She was glad that she hadn't gotten into her workout and started sweating because he was licking her in places she never thought he'd give attention to. He was a wonderful lover, and she realized what she had been missing for so long. He rubbed her body just right and even licked the milk from her breasts. She enjoyed his masterful foreplay and took the liberty of helping him put on the condom. She was surprised at how free she felt with him. She wasn't ashamed of her body the way she was with Devon.

When she climaxed, she collapsed on his chest, and he flipped her over and finished up. He groaned and breathed deeply, and she knew he had gotten his too. She looked over at the clock. Their hour session had been over thirty minutes ago. She smiled and closed her eyes and drifted off to sleep.

A little while later, she felt Ray ease out of bed, and she then heard the shower. She went back to sleep.

***

"Baby," Ray said, shaking her.

Leila opened her eyes and blinked. She wasn't sure how long she had been asleep.

"Your phone was ringing," he said, handing her purse to her.

"Aw, thanks," she said, digging around in her purse. She found her phone and looked at her missed calls. It was the store.

"Is everything okay?" Ray asked.

"Yeah, just gotta call the store," she said, sitting up.

"Take your time. I gotta get back to work," he said, standing.

"You still have appointments?" She didn't know he had more clients to see. And she was shocked he wasn't asking her to leave.

"Yeah, 'til six."

"I can go."

"No, I want you to stay."

"Are you sure?" she asked.

He walked back over to her. "Of course I'm sure. Make your call. I'll be right upstairs," he said and gave her another kiss. She smiled and watched him leave.

Chapter Thirteen

"Renee, it's me, Leila."

"Where the hell are you, girl?"

"Guess."

"You must be with Devon," Renee said. Leila could hear her disappointment leaking through the earpiece.

"Nope. I am not with Devon."

"At the salon again?"

"Nope." Leila smiled, pulling the covers over her naked body.

"Well then, where?"

"At Ray's."

"Okay," Renee said.

"And I am naked in his bed."

"No, you are not!" Renee screamed.

"Yes, I am."

"I thought you said you and Satan—I mean, Devon—were getting back together."

"Well, girlfriend, I lied."

"You are not moving on, Lei. You are shitting me."

"I am moving on. I'm not playing games with Devon. Even if this is nothing between Ray and me, I am living my life for me, and I'm not gonna let Devon come back when it's convenient for him and turn my world upside down. If he wants to be with Michelle or whomever else, I don't care."

"You go, girl," Renee said. "I just want you to be sure of what you are doing, Miss Thing, because that Ray is a sexy mother-shut-yo'-mouth, and you said that a lot of women come in and out of there."

"You know what? Life is too short to stress, and if he is on some bull, you know I will know, so just wish me luck and let's see how it goes."

"All right, then. I take it you won't be back to the store today?"

"If you don't mind."

"Nope, I'm good."

"Thanks. Now let me call Devon to see if he can get Deja for me tonight."

"Good luck with that," Renee said.

"Tell me about it."

"Be careful, and call me if you need me."

"I will," Leila said, and they hung up. She took a deep breath and called Devon.

He answered on the second ring. "Hey, baby, what's up?" he said cheerfully. Leila instantly felt like shit.

"Hey, Devon, how are you?"

"I am outstanding," he replied.

"Listen, can you pick Deja up this evening?"

"Sure, not a problem. Where are you going to be?"

"I'm gonna go do some shopping. You don't mind, do you?"

"Naw, that's cool. Your place or mine tonight?" he asked.

"I'll be by to get the baby tonight," she said. She heard the tremor in her voice.

"Okay, then my place is cool," he said. She didn't want to get into it with him over the phone, so she agreed.

"I'll see you later," she said and hung up quickly. She heard him say, "I love you," just before the call disconnected.

She put her phone on the nightstand and looked around Ray's room. He had good taste, she thought. She got up and wrapped the sheet around her and looked out the window at the view. It was even more beautiful from his bedroom. She stood there and gazed out the window until the sound of music coming through the partially open bedroom door brought her back.

She went across the room and climbed back into his king-sized bed. It had a mahogany platform that was low to the floor, with matching nightstands. It looked totally opposite of her bedroom, but it was very nice. She looked up at the exposed brick wall behind the bed and admired the decor. She was curious, so she went into his bathroom. To her surprise, it was massive. He had a separate shower and a huge garden tub with jets. The his-and-hers vanities and tiled floors were earth tone with accents of black in the granite.

Leila went back into the bedroom and sat on the edge of the bed. The music stopped and she heard voices, but she couldn't make out exactly what was being said. She relaxed until she heard, "You know you want me. I don't see why you keep playing." She recognized the voice. It was Christa. That trick was throwing herself at Ray.

Leila felt territorial, but she didn't move until she heard Ray say, "Come on, Christa. It's time for you to go."

"Ray," Leila yelled. Within moments, he stuck his head in the door. She was nervous and wished she hadn't done that, but when she saw the smile on his face, she knew it was okay.

"Yeah?" he said. She could tell he wanted to laugh, but he didn't.

"Can you get me some water? I'm a little thirsty," she said with a smirk.

"Babe, can you come and get it? Because I'm with a client." He winked.

"I have to come and get it?" she whined.

"I am sorta busy," he said. He motioned for her to come out, and she got up, wrapped the sheet around her, and walked out. Christa's mouth dropped when she saw Leila.

"Oh, hi, Christa. How was your workout today?" Leila went to the kitchen and grabbed a bottle of water from the refrigerator while Christa stood there with her mouth open. She opened the fridge again, grabbed another bottle, and walked back into the living area. "Here you go, Christa," she said, handing it to her. "It was nice seeing you again," she said and went back into the bedroom. She stood by the door and listened.

"Oh, so you don't fuck your clients? I could have sworn she was a client, Ray. You fucking the big one?"

"You're right. She was a client, and now she's not."

"You know what? I give up. I don't want your punk ass anyway. I'll see you next week," Christa said and stormed out.

"That went well," she heard Ray say.

Leila ran and jumped into the bed like she hadn't been listening. Ray walked into the room and jumped on the bed, and they burst into laughter.

"'I don't want your punk ass anyway,'" he said, mocking Christa, and they continued laughing.

"So, I'm no longer a client?" Leila asked.

"I have a guy I can refer you to. He's good, and I know you'll continue to do well," he said.

She didn't know whether to take him seriously. "You gon' dump me just like that?" She still wanted him to be her trainer. She trusted him and wasn't comfortable with going to another trainer.

"You know I can't continue to be your trainer if we're together. That's bad for business."

"You can't just dump me. Need I remind you that we have a contract?" she said, sitting up. She wasn't about to let him just push her off to a new trainer.

"Oh, yeah, we do have a contract," he said, rubbing his chin.

"Yeah, Mr. Throw Me Away."

"Well, how about we just rip up the contract and you work out *with* me from now on?" he said, smiling.

"Oh, it's like that? You wanna work me out in other ways?" she asked seductively. She felt so comfortable with him. It was like they had been together longer than just that day.

"Yes, I would, if you don't mind."

"I don't mind," she said, and they kissed. They were ready to get started until a knock came on the door. "Who is that?" Leila asked.

"Oh, baby, I almost forgot my four o'clock," Ray said, getting up.

"You have another client?" she asked, disappointed that he couldn't stay with her.

"Yes, and I have a five, and then I'll be done," he said, readjusting himself. The bulge in his pants showed Leila his excitement.

"Aw, can't you cancel?"

"Hold that thought," he said and made a dash to the door.

He came back into the room a few minutes later and got another kiss, then handed her the remote and suggested she watch a little television while she waited. She turned on the tube, flipped through the channels, and landed on the HGTV network. She left it there and got comfortable. She dozed off and was in a deep sleep when she felt warm kisses on her arm.

"Hey, you," Ray said when she opened her eyes.

"Hey," she responded, trying to focus her eyes.

"Are you hungry?" he asked.

"Yes. What time is it?" She yawned and stretched. Her body felt a bit sore, and it wasn't from working out.

"It's ten after six," he said, getting up and going into his closet.

Leila reached over, turned on the lamp on the nightstand, and looked at her phone. She was relieved that she had no calls from Devon. She sat up and watched Ray pull out clothes from his closet.

"You're done for the day?"

"Yes, ma'am, and I want you to get up and shower because I am taking you to dinner."

"I won't argue with you on that," she said, getting up. Although she had dropped a few pounds, she wasn't comfortable walking around naked in front of him. "Do you have a robe or something I can put on?" she asked, sitting on the side of the bed, holding the sheet tight.

"Why?" he teasingly. "I know what your body looks like, so why are you getting shy on me?"

"I'm not. I just wanna cover up. Please?" she said.

"Why? It's only us. Besides, I wanna watch you walk into the bathroom."

"I'd rather you didn't," she said, turning her head.

"Listen, you have to relax, okay? I want you to feel comfortable around me, and I want to look at you," he said, coming over and sitting next to her on the bed.

"Trust me, you don't wanna look at my body. It's nothing like Christa's or Karen's—"

Ray stopped her. "You are Leila. I know that your body is not like Christa's or whoever's. I know that you have stretch marks here," he said, pointing to her stomach, "and I saw your roll right here," he said, reaching around her back, "and I don't have a problem with the way these jiggle," he said, shaking her thighs. Leila laughed. "I feel for you and only you. The day I saw you in the bookstore, you were fine, and you are fine now, so cut a brother some slack," he said.

She felt better. Not completely confident, but not as nervous. "Okay, but if I blind you, don't be trying to sue a sista," she said and got up.

She let the sheet drop to the floor and went into the bathroom. She turned on the water in the shower and waited a few moments for it to warm up. Ray came into the bathroom and gave her a fresh towel and looked inside one of the vanity drawers for a new toothbrush. She saw about ten toothbrushes.

"Why do you have so many toothbrushes? Do you have that many women sleep over?" she asked.

"Ha-ha. The thing is, smarty-pants, I have clients in and out of here all the time, and sometimes after a workout, the breath tends to act up. So I have a box in the hall bathroom. I took a few of them out and put them here for other guests. There are just as many left as the day I put them there. I am not that kind of guy."

"Well, Ray, forgive me. Sometimes I just speak my mind."

"It's cool. I'm not offended."

"Good," she said and stepped into the steamy shower. "You wouldn't happen to have a blow dryer, would you?" The steam would cause havoc to her hair, and she'd look crazy after the shower.

"Now that is something I don't have," he said, stepping in with her.

They caressed each other and made more steam than the hot water. When they were done and finally stepped out of the shower, Leila could have screamed at her reflection in the mirror. She had on no makeup, and although her hair was long, the moisture drew it up, and the natural curls took form.

She dried her skin and asked Ray to bring her gym bag from upstairs. She had a change of clothes and her hairbrush and makeup bag. She put lotion on her skin and put on her underwear. She brushed her hair back and put it in a ponytail, something she hated to do, but it was the best she could do under the circumstances. She applied a generous amount of eye shadow to enhance her eyes and a nice gloss to make sure she looked presentable for dinner. When she came out of the bathroom, Ray was standing in front of his armoire in his boxers. *Damn, his back looks good.*

She wondered if this was a dream. Was this something that was going to go somewhere, or was this just going to be a fling? She stood there and watched him for a moment before she realized she was staring. When he turned around and saw her watching him, she turned her head in embarrassment.

"What?" he asked.

"Nothing," she said. She walked over to her bag on the bed and took out her sweater and jeans.

"You were thinking something," he pressed.

"No, I wasn't," she said, lying.

He walked over and embraced her from behind. "I would like for this to go somewhere.

I have fantasized about you, about us, and I thought this moment would never come. I would like you to always be honest with me, no matter what. I don't care how silly it may be or whatever. If I ask you what you're thinking, it's all right to tell me. If I ask you how you feel, hey, I really wanna know how you feel."

"Okay, I got you. I just can't get over how fine you look, and you wanna be with me. I know it's foolish to say, but I'm kinda nervous, you know?"

"Let me tell you this: if at any point I make you feel less than a woman, or if you ever feel anything other than good feelings with me, tell me, and I will fix it. I like you, Leila, more than I've liked a woman in a long while, and I am anxious to see how this will go, okay? So relax and trust me."

"Okay, I will try to relax. I've just been with a man who adored me one day, and then as soon as one thing changed about me, he changed on me. I know that there are beautiful women out there, and you come into contact with tons of them. If we're together, I have to be sure that it's me you want."

"Let's just take it one day at a time. Can you do that for me?" he said, touching her face.

"Yes, I can," she said with a smile.

Chapter Fourteen

Ray stood at the door of Leila's Armada, freezing because he didn't want to say goodbye. It was already after ten, and she had told him five times that she had to get to Devon's to pick up Deja, but he still didn't want to say good night. He finally gave her one last kiss, shut her door, and went upstairs feeling like a million bucks. He poured himself a shot of scotch and turned on some music. He saw Leila's gym bag by the door and smiled. He was happy that he had told her how he felt, and he hoped to spend more time with her.

Still smiling, he changed into sweats and a T-shirt. He felt like a young boy with his first crush. He thought back to the day when he first saw her at the bookstore sitting behind the counter and acting like she was this married woman and off-limits. He chuckled when he thought about her saying, "I'll see if my husband would like to come." After getting to know her and spending time training her, she had finally shared with him the real deal about her and her failed marriage. From the moment she told him about Devon leaving her when she was pregnant, he wanted to protect her.

He'd started to think of her on the regular from then on. Every session they had, he grew fonder of her. He'd go to the bookstore at least four times a week. Most times, he didn't buy a thing, just pretended to look for something. He started to ask more questions about her personal life, like her favorite color, her favorite movie, and what food she liked. Anything to give him an idea of what she was about. The more they talked, the more he was interested. And one day, she came for a session, and he wanted to touch her. He wanted to kiss her. He realized that he was physically attracted to her.

The day had finally come, and he had made his move. He was a bit apprehensive, though, because of the conversation they had about her and Devon and how she was considering getting back with him. He knew she was over her ex, or at least he hoped she was. He tried to relax and not let it get to him. He would just take it day by day and see how things went. He was sure that he and Leila would be good together. He would treat her the way she longed to be treated.

He picked up his cell phone and dialed her number, but didn't press the TALK button to connect the call. He was putting the phone back on his nightstand when it rang. The number on the caller ID looked familiar, but he couldn't remember who it belonged to. He waited a few seconds and then went ahead and answered it.

"Hey, this is Ray," he said.

"Hey, how are you?" a woman's voice said.

"I'm fine," he said, wondering who it was on the other end.

"That's good," she said.

Ray didn't respond. He was trying to recognize the voice.

"Are you still there?" she asked.

"Yeah, yeah, I'm here." *Who the hell is this?*

"What are you getting into tonight?" she asked.

"Nothing too much. I just got in from having dinner."

"Would you like to get into me tonight?"

"I don't wanna get into anyone I don't know. I'm trying, but I must be honest. I don't recognize your voice."

"This is Karen," she said.

Ray hated that he answered the phone. "Oh, hey, Karen. What's going on?"

"Nothing too much. I was just trying to see you tonight. I mean, I know it was foul for me to drop by your place earlier, and again, I do apologize for coming by unannounced. I just had such a good time with you the other night, and I was hoping we can get together soon and do it again."

"You know I have a tight schedule. I don't do too much during the week because my earliest appointment is normally at five, so I'll have to let you know." He hoped she'd take the hint and realize that was a brush-off.

"How about Friday? We could see a movie or get some dinner?" she said, sounding a bit desperate.

Ray would normally just be honest, but he didn't want to hurt her feelings. "You know what? That sounds good. Let me call you Friday morning to let you know if I can free up some time. I usually take clients at the twenty-four-hour fitness center, and I may have to get with you later than dinner or movie time."

"Whatever you can work out. Just call me."

"I will," he said, knowing that he had no intention of doing that.

"Have a good night," she said softly.

Ray felt bad. He knew Karen was a nice woman, maybe even a good woman, but she wasn't the woman he was looking for. He hung up and took his phone over to the charger and plugged it in.

He wished he had told her the truth and not led her to believe that he'd go out with her on Friday. He wanted to call her back and just tell her the real, but he wasn't in the mood to deal with that situation right then. He wanted to talk to Leila. Since she had not called him yet, he figured he'd kill some time by running on the treadmill. She said she would call him once she picked up her baby from Devon's, so he'd just wait.

He wasn't too happy that she had to go by her ex's house, but he knew that he couldn't do anything about him being her daughter's father. He just wished things were different. He wished that he had met her before she got married. He hoped that Leila would be strong and not go back.

Ray got on the treadmill and put on his headset. He ran his normal two miles and decided to do one more. He felt so energetic and hyped that he ran the extra mile without difficulty. He finished and grabbed a towel from the stack on the shelf. He wiped his face and stretched. He was still full of energy, so he pulled out the mat and did fifty push-ups and one hundred sit-ups. Then he went over to the mini fridge, grabbed a bottle of water, and drank it straight. After a few moments of calming down and getting himself together, he grabbed a few sanitary wipes and wiped everything down.

He went downstairs and hopped into the shower. After he showered and brushed his teeth, he put on a pair of boxers and checked the clock. It was almost one a.m., and he hadn't gotten a call from Leila. He checked his cell phone and saw two missed calls, but the number wasn't one he recognized. He didn't bother listening to his voicemail. Instead, he got into bed, made sure his alarm was set, and grabbed his cordless phone to call Leila.

He dialed her cell phone first. It went straight to her voicemail, and that made him nervous. He hung up without leaving her a message. He thought for a few moments and finally dialed her house. He waited for three rings before he hung up. He got angry. All he could think of was her in Devon's arms after she had left him. How could she look at him and lie to his face? Why did she make him think she was interested in him? Why did she tell him that she was ready to move on if she really wasn't?

He decided that he'd give up. He wasn't in the business of letting women hurt him. He had vowed that Katrina would be the last woman who would ever hurt him. She was beautiful, and every man wanted her. He had met her at the gym, and his first thought was, *damn, I gotta have that*. He stepped to her, and she told him that she had a man, so he stepped off. Less than a week later, she was in the parking lot of the gym, crying in her car.

When he saw her, he tapped on her window and asked her if she was okay. When she said no, he asked her if there was something he could do. She'd said, "Kill my ex-boyfriend," and they started kicking it from there. Everywhere they went, men were always trying to get with her. Even in front of Ray, dudes would step to her. He tried to trust Katrina, but it was hard because she got so much attention.

Every time he'd turn around, a dude was in her face. He tried to deal with it, but he was insecure. She assured him that she was in love with him and didn't want anyone but him, but he couldn't relax. He'd call her every hour on the hour, and he basically kept tabs on her. He was so worried about her being unfaithful that he couldn't enjoy the relationship. Although she tried to assure him that she was true, he always felt that some dude would be in her ear with some bullshit and she'd fall for it.

After a year, he finally calmed down. He had no reason to believe Katrina was untrue because they did everything and went everywhere together. He learned to relax and enjoy his relationship, and he stopped stressing her and started acting like a normal boyfriend. He didn't call her fifteen times a day, and he didn't ask her twenty questions every time he walked up on her and a guy was in her face.

He thanked God for blessing him with a woman who was not only beautiful but smart and faithful. He fell in love with Katrina, and after two years of dating her, he finally proposed. They were engaged and happy and had plans to open a fitness center together. Things were perfect, or so he thought.

One day, a new client at the gym saw him talking to Katrina. During their session, his client asked him how he knew Katrina, and Ray told him that she was his fiancée.

"Oh, really?" the guy said with a surprised look on his face.

Ray asked him, "What's up, dawg? What's that supposed to mean?"

The guy just laughed and didn't say anything.

At the end of their session, the client said, "Look, I ain't trying to fuck up a happy home, but your girl is foul, believe that."

"Come on, dude. You gotta come with it all. What's up?"

"My boy hitting that on a regular," the guy said. "Ask your girl about Jay," he said and walked away.

Ray was devastated. When he thought about it, he realized that anytime she had been around when the guy came in for a session, she disappeared. She had to know him. Why else would she have bounced like that? Angry and hurt, and he went on a rampage through the gym, looking for Katrina. She was nowhere to be found.

He called her back-to-back on her cell phone, and she didn't pick up. He tried to reach her all evening. After his shift, he decided to roll by her spot to talk to her. When he got there, her roommate said she wasn't home and she hadn't seen her. Ray went home. When he got there, Katrina was sitting in the hall on the floor, waiting for him. She looked scared, like she thought he was going to go off, but he wasn't as angry as he was earlier. He was calm.

He opened the door and didn't say anything. After a few moments, she came inside.

"I was gonna tell you, but I didn't know how," she said softly.

"Tell me what, Kat? That you're fucking some dude named Jay?" he asked her. His earlier calm disappeared.

"I know that Mike told you about what he thinks he knows about Jay and me, but I swear that I haven't been with him since you and I *got engaged. I swear we were over a long time ago," she cried.*

"Don't play me. Tell me the fucking truth. This guy was in my face, telling me how you're fucking this dude on a regular. Why would he say that if that bullshit has been over?" he yelled.

"Ray, please. You know I love you more than anything. I wouldn't lie to you."

He didn't believe her.

After an hour of arguing and going back and forth, he gave in, gave her the benefit of the doubt, and they made love. That night he prayed to God and asked him to let Katrina be the woman she said she was and for him to be able to trust her. Things were quiet and good between them for the next couple of days, like nothing was wrong.

A few nights after, Ray found out the worst. They were cuddled up in the bed, and he felt Katrina get up. She went into the front room, and after a while, he got up and went to see what she was doing. The light was on in the hall bathroom, and he eased up close to the door. He could hear Katrina on the phone.

"Jay, you have to be patient. I am gonna tell him," she said.

He didn't want to hear any more, but he couldn't walk away. He listened to her say how she was going to break up with him and make her thing with Jay perfect and right.

Ray couldn't believe it. She had lied to him, and he let her get away with it. It hurt. He went back into his bedroom and lay in the dark, waiting for his unfaithful princess to get back into bed. When she got back into bed, he didn't say anything. She snuggled close to him, and he let silent tears run down the side of his face. He moved a little, and Katrina readjusted herself.

"I love you," she whispered.

When he heard those three words come out of her lying lips, he exploded. "Get out!" he roared.

Katrina's head popped up. "What?" she asked. He could see her wide eyes in the darkness.

"Get out," he thundered. "Get the fuck up and get yo' sneaky, lying ass out of my bed."

"What in the hell is wrong with you?" she yelled back at him.

"I'm going to say this one time only, and I don't want to hear shit from you. I am not a fool, so get up and get your stuff and get out."

Katrina jumped up and turned on the lights. She started to gather her things. "I don't know what's wrong with you, but when you come to your senses, call me."

"Trust me, Katrina, I won't be calling you."

"What is wrong? What happened, baby? Why are you acting so crazy?" she cried. Her body shook like a leaf in a Chicago winter.

"You gon' act like you just didn't get your trifling ass up and go into my bathroom and call your other man on your cell phone?" he yelled. *"You actually gon' stand there and look me in my eye and ask me what's wrong with me? What the hell is wrong with you is the question. Now with all due respect, and before this gets out of hand up in here, you need to make your exit."*

She hadn't wasted any time getting out of his loft. After that night, he made it a point to not say another word to her. He didn't even ask for his ring back. He just never spoke to her again. They would see each other at the gym, and he would walk by her as if she were invisible. She tried for months to talk to him, but he simply ignored her and made it a point not to look in her direction. That was one of the reasons he had converted his loft into a gym. He got tired of running into Katrina. He wanted to avoid her at all costs. It had been almost six years since their relationship ended.

He knew that not all women were the same, but he made it a point to stay away from the gorgeous ones. The women who got extra attention were not the type of women he went after. He was turned off by women like Christa, Katrina, and all the model-type wannabes he trained. None of them did anything for him. Women like them were simply trouble and a guaranteed headache.

When he met Leila, his heart had skipped a beat. She was pretty enough, but her beauty was inside, and that was what he wanted for himself. He wanted to be with a woman who would be his woman and his only. He wanted a woman who a man might not glance at twice. Not that he wanted an ugly woman. He wanted an average woman. That was what he thought he saw in Leila, but after spending the day with her and making love to her, he felt otherwise. She was even more attractive than Katrina and Christa. He just hoped that he would not have to compete with Devon to have her. He wanted her for himself.

Chapter Fifteen

Leila finally made it out of Devon's condo. She had given him a million and one reasons she couldn't stay with him that night and had even lied so she could get out of there. She'd told him that he could come over and stay with her the next night. She wanted to tell him it was really over, but she knew if she did, he would have never let her get out the door. She pulled up at her house at a quarter 'til one, and even though it was late, she wanted to call Ray. She knew she wouldn't be able to fall asleep without hearing his voice.

She hurried inside to get herself situated so she could call him. She put Deja to bed and ran into her room and took off her clothes. Before she could get in her bed and get comfortable, her phone rang. It was Devon, calling to make sure she and the baby were home safe. She tried to not rush him, but when he started talking about their relationship and their marriage, she was ready to hang up in his face. Her other line rang, and the caller ID showed it was Ray. She tried to make Devon get off, but he kept talking. Before she could answer the other line, Ray hung up.

"Listen, Devon, please. I am tired, and I have to get up early in the morning. Let me call you tomorrow."

"How about I pick you up for lunch tomorrow? We can get a room like we used to do when we first got married and order some room service and, you know, do what we do," he said.

"Come on now." She frowned. "You are moving too fast. You want to do too much." She was no longer interested in Devon and his antics.

"Okay, okay, you're right. How about just lunch?"

"Lunch is fine. Just, please, Devon, I am exhausted."

"Okay, baby, get some sleep. I love you."

"Good night," Leila said and hung up.

She dialed Ray's number and got into bed while she waited for him to answer. He picked up on the fourth ring.

"Hello," he said. His voice was low, almost muffled.

"Hey, are you sleeping?" she asked.

"Yeah, but I'm good."

"I'm sorry I'm calling so late, but Devon was difficult, and my battery was dead on my cell phone, so I couldn't call you from the truck."

"No, it's okay. How is your little one?"

"She is fine. In there, sleeping her butt off. She is so sweet, Ray."

"I can imagine. I can't wait to see her again."

"Really?" Leila asked, surprised.

"Yes, she is beautiful."

"She gets it from her momma," Leila said, joking.

"She sure does."

"Well, listen, I don't want to keep you up. I just wanted to call you to let you know I was thinking of you and that I made it home safely."

"You aren't keeping me up. I wanna be up. I wish I could be near you."

"Me too," she said, squeezing her pillow tight.

"Can I see you tomorrow?"

"I don't know. I have to be at my store all day, and then I have to get Deja afterward."

"You can bring your baby along. I just wanna see you, Leila."

"Okay, that will be fine, if you don't mind me bringing Deja along."

"Why would I mind? I know you're a mother."

"I know, but not too many men wanna be bothered with another man's child."

"I'm not your average man."

"You're right about that," she said.

"What do you mean, Ms. Leila?"

"Well, for starters, you're not the man I imagined you were when I first met you."

"What type of man did you think I was?"

"Pardon me, but I thought you'd be an egotistical player. Never in a million years would I have thought you'd be so humble or interested in an average, plus-size woman like me."

"I'm happy that you were wrong about me."

"I am too. I'm still a little afraid, but I'm gonna do what you asked and just take it one day at a time."

"And that's all we can do. I'm still a little apprehensive about you and Devon, but—"

"Hey, you don't have to worry about Devon and me, okay? That is already a done deal. I just have to finalize my divorce."

"Which includes getting him to sign the papers, remember?"

"That's true. But don't worry. He will sign them."

"If you say so."

"Ray, please don't worry."

"I'm not worried, but please, Leila, for me to be happy and continue to be sane, I only require your honesty. Don't tell me one thing if there i something else. I will respect you more if you're always honest with me."

"And I ask the same of you. If you wake up one day and I'm not the one, don't make me think that it's all good. Just let me know."

"Trust, I've been there, so I wouldn't do that."

"With who?" she asked, curious.

"That is another story. I'll share it with you one day."

"Okay, but trust that I'll remind you."

"You're a woman. Of course you will," he said, and they laughed.

Ray yawned, and Leila knew she had to get off the phone. Even though her baby slept the entire night now, she woke up at six a.m. She had to get some sleep.

"I'll let you get some sleep, but I will definitely see you tomorrow," she said, reaching over and turning on her alarm.

"Call me tomorrow."

"I will. Good night," she said.

"Good night to you," he said, and they hung up.

Leila smiled and turned out the lamp on her nightstand. She couldn't remember feeling this excited about a man before. Devon was the first man she had fallen in love with, and she didn't have much experience with men. She'd had a couple of boyfriends in high school, but nothing serious. Then she went to college and met Devon.

They had met at a party, and after one dance, he followed her around everywhere she went. She remembered telling her friends that he was stalking her. She couldn't shake him back then, so she was really hurt and confused when he turned on her. When he started to treat her cold and acted like he didn't give a damn about her, she was devastated. He would walk out on her when she would get hysterical and leave her by herself to calm down, even when she was pregnant.

She thought back on how she would call him and he wouldn't answer. How he was supposed to meet her at a doctor's appointment and he wouldn't show. When she'd call him and ask him why, he'd give her any old excuse and act as if he didn't care. She'd had her baby's ultrasound pictures hanging on the fridge at her house an entire month before he even noticed. He'd briefly stop by just to so-called check on her or because she had begged him to come and do chores like mopping or anything that required lifting. He'd come over and help her with the laundry after she'd beg him for days, so she didn't have to go up and down the steps.

By the time she was eight months pregnant, she had needed him to move back home to help her, but he refused and would answer her calls only when he was ready. It usually took at least eight or nine phone calls for him to pick up. When she went into labor, she had to call Renee because he wouldn't answer. Her water broke and, of course, she panicked. She didn't know what to do, so she called Devon, crying on his voicemail, telling him that she thought she was in labor and to call her back right away. After ten minutes, her contractions started, and they were strong.

Leila had sat on her porch, frantic and unsure whether she should drive herself or call a cab. She was so nervous and scared she couldn't think. What man in his right mind wouldn't pick up his phone when he knew his wife was close to her delivery date?

She called Devon again and again until she finally thought of Renee. When she called, Renee told her to hang tight, and she'd be right there. She lived about thirty minutes away but made it to Leila's in twenty minutes. Leila was still on the porch, sweating, shaking, and crying, with her cell phone still in her hand. Renee ran inside and got her keys and purse and rushed her to the hospital.

When they admitted Leila, her contractions were three minutes apart. She gave birth in the labor room because there was no time to make it to the delivery room. By the time Devon finally called her back, she was resting in her room with her newborn baby. When he got to the hospital, he felt like shit for missing his daughter's birth. He told Leila that he was in meetings all day and that was the reason he didn't answer. She just looked at him and didn't say a word. She knew he was lying. When she had been on the porch calling him, she had called his office, and his assistant said he wasn't in.

When he picked Deja up out of the little bassinet, he sat down and broke down crying. He made promises to Leila that he wouldn't leave her side and that he was going to get his act together and come home and be a father to Deja and a husband to her. Fake promises.

He vowed that he would be a better man. That lasted for six weeks. He had moved back home to help her with Deja.

After her six-week checkup, when she was able to move around and handle the baby better, Devon went back to his old behavior—not coming when he said he would and not answering his phone when he didn't want to answer his phone. Leila went back to crying and begging, and Devon went back to not caring. They'd have a good week or a good few days, then they went back to a horrible week and a horrible few days

Leila would plead and beg, and Devon would lie and make empty promises. She gave him chance after chance. She just couldn't get over him. She allowed him to spend the night when he wanted to, and she gave him her body whenever he wanted it. She held on to her hope that her husband would come home and be with her.

Then he told her that he wanted a divorce. He told her multiple times that he would file for a divorce, but he never did. He would tell her on Monday that he didn't see a chance for them to get back together, and then on Thursday, he would tell her he loved her and he was sorry for putting her through hell.

Now Leila was strong and ready to reestablish her life. She finally had enough sense to shut Devon down. But all of a sudden, his intentions were genuine. He was showing heartfelt interest in getting back with her. She hadn't seen or heard about Michelle, and he was home more, answered his phone every time she called, and wouldn't hesitate to be right there for her when she needed him.

He kept saying that he didn't want the divorce, and she was starting to believe him. Although she knew she couldn't trust Devon and she didn't really want him back, she was caught up in the idea of them getting back together. She felt that, for the sake of the baby, if he wanted to come back, she should let him, even though deep down that wasn't what she sincerely desired. She loved him, yes, but the romantic love for him was gone.

She no longer missed him when he wasn't around. She no longer cared if he called or stopped by. She was at the point in her life where living without him was something she could live with. It wasn't like that before. She was relieved that she no longer cried every day. She was finally at peace with him no longer being in her life. So she went out and did it. She filed for divorce so she could be free to be happy.

And now he wanna come back, she thought.

Chapter Sixteen

Ray got up at four thirty with no problem. He showered and brushed his teeth while he bobbed his head to the music that filled his loft. He knew his neighbors were cursing him out for listening to music that early and so loud, but he didn't care. He was ready to get the day started because he was anxious to see Leila again. His first appointment was there on time, and he got started right away. The day's sessions went by quickly, and before he knew it, it was five o'clock and he was opening the door for his last appointment. Or so he thought.

When he opened the door, Katrina was there. Ray had to blink twice. He stood there staring at her, unable to speak. He could not believe his eyes.

"Hi, Ray. Can I come in?" she asked.

He frowned. "What do you want?" he asked.

"I need to talk to you. I need to talk to somebody," she said and started crying. "I have nowhere else to go, Ray, please," she said, sobbing.

He sighed and let her in and closed the door. She sat down, and he glanced at the clock. Mia, his next appointment, would be there any minute.

"Look, Kat, I'm sorry, but I have to work. My five o'clock is on the way."

"Can I just hang out here for a while? I promise I won't get in the way. I just . . . I—"

There was a knock on the door. Mia had arrived.

"Listen, you can wait here, but understand that whatever it is, I can't help you," he said and opened the door.

Mia came in and saw Katrina sitting on the couch, crying. She paused. "Do we need to reschedule?" she asked Ray.

"No, come on in. Just go on up, and I'll be there in a sec." She went upstairs, and he turned his attention to Katrina. She looked bad, not at all the way he remembered her. He wasn't sure what her dilemma was, but he was definitely sure he didn't want to get involved. "I'll be an hour, so sit tight. If you're hungry or need something to drink, help yourself."

"Okay," she said softly and nodded.

He turned to go upstairs and heard her call his name. He turned to look at her. "Yes?"

"Thank you," she said, sniffing.

"Don't worry," he said and went on upstairs.

It seemed like the session with Mia took forever. When it was finally over, he went down to let her out and found Katrina sleeping on the sofa. He let Mia out and sat looking at his ex. Her clothes were stained, and they looked oversized, like they weren't hers. Her handbag looked like it had clothing items in it. He wondered what in the hell was going on with her. She was sleeping hard, so he didn't wake her. She looked like she needed rest.

He stood up and went back upstairs to wipe everything down like he normally did after every session. He went back down and went into the kitchen and saw that Katrina had helped herself to a sandwich and left all the fixings on the counter. He cleared away everything and went back to check on her. She was still asleep. He took a deep breath and asked himself why he let her in. He got his cell phone and called Leila. It wasn't a good idea for her and Deja to come over until he figured out what was going on with Katrina.

"Hey, Leila," he said when she answered.

"Hey, you. What's going on?" she sang. He loved the happiness he heard in her voice.

"Listen, something has come up, and I may have to see you tomorrow."

Leila was silent.

"Leila, baby, are you there?"

"I'm here, Rayshon," she said, now with disappointment in her tone, something he didn't want to hear. "Why, what's going on?"

"I'm sorry, but an old friend of mine is in trouble, and I have to help."

"Oh, okay. I'm sorry. Is there anything I can do?"

"No, but thanks, and I promise I will call you a little later."

"I'll be at home."

"Take care, and I'll call you back soon."

"Just take care of your friend."

"Thanks for understanding," he said, and they hung up.

Ray went to shower and change. When he came back, Katrina was still sleeping. He didn't bother her. He just let her sleep. It was close to ten when she finally opened her eyes. He was sitting in a chair watching television with the volume down low when she sat up and stretched.

"Did you sleep well?" he asked.

"Yes. What time is it?"

"It's a quarter 'til ten."

"Oh, it's that late? You let me sleep, Ray?" she asked, her eyes wide.

He was just as surprised as she was. "Yes, I did. You looked like you needed some rest."

"I am very tired."

"Are you hungry?"

"I'm starving," she said and stood. "Can I use the bathroom?"

"You know where it is." He got up and went to the kitchen to heat up some chicken, rice, and steamed vegetables. He set the plate of food on the coffee table along with a bottle of water and waited until she came out of the bathroom. She sat back on the sofa, and he pointed at the food and water. She opened the water bottle and took a swallow.

"Kat, what's the deal? Why are you here?" he asked when she finally put the empty plate on the table.

"I tried calling you twice last night, and I left you a message, but you didn't call me back. I figured you wouldn't, so I came to talk to you face-to-face."

"About what? What do you wanna talk to me about?"

"I know I'm the last person you want to see right now, but I'm in a jam. I need a place to crash 'til I can save up some money to get me a place. I've been living in my car for the last couple of weeks. I don't have any place to go."

"What about your mom's? Go to her house," he suggested. He knew her mom well, and he knew there was no way she would have Katrina living in her car.

"Ray, my mom is dead," she said. Tears rolled down her face.

"What? When? What happened?" he asked. He had no idea she'd passed.

"About three months ago. She had gotten really sick a year ago, and I moved her in with me to take care of her. When she was living with us, things got worse for her, and it caused problems with me and . . ." She hesitated then continued. "Jay just wasn't happy to help me with my sick mother, and we argued and argued. When my momma died, I was depressed, and he wasn't there for me. It was like he didn't care. Anyway, things didn't get any better, and about a month ago, he put me out. I stayed at Yvonne's, but I messed that up too, and she threw me out. She wouldn't let me come in and get my things because of some shit about me supposedly sleeping with her man. I didn't. I swear on my life, Rayshon. He wanted me, and she knew he was after me. I have been just down and out since she threw me out. When Momma died, she had no insurance, so I wiped out my savings burying her. I am broke.

"I'm gon' lose my job if I don't get it together," she said, sobbing. "I was in a motel for a couple of days, but I have no money, Ray. My car note is due, and I am behind on everything. My life is so out of control. I just need somebody to help me."

Ray got up and went to get her a tissue. When he came back, he sat down beside her and held her. He felt bad for her, but he was in no position to help her. Not the way she wanted him to.

He couldn't let her stay with him, and loaning her money was out of the question. He could probably put her up in a motel for a while, but that was all he would do.

"Listen, Katrina, I am sorry about your mom. I will help you, but you cannot stay here. I am involved with someone, and I don't want any drama and confusion. I'll help you, but you have to stay away from here. We aren't friends anymore, but I can't leave you out there like that. I'll get you a room for a couple weeks and get things straight with your car so you don't lose your transportation, but that's it. That's all I can do for you."

"That's fine. Anything will help me at this point." She looked at him gratefully. "I promise I will pay you back every dime when I get on my feet."

Ray turned away from her. Emotions and feelings he didn't want to examine were trying to creep up. "You don't have to pay me back."

He went to his desk and got his checkbook. He asked how much she owed on her car note, and she told him. He wrote out a check to her finance company for the two months she owed and handed it to her. Then he told her that a guy he used to train ran a hotel, and he was sure he could get her in for a few days. Katrina moved to a chair next to the desk and listened while he made a phone call. He worked out a deal for one month and gave Katrina's information so she could check in without him.

"The hotel is nice, and they serve breakfast every morning. Here is some cash to get you going." He pulled a couple hundred dollars out of his wallet and handed it to her. He had done way more than enough. $1,500 more, to be exact. *If that's not enough, oh well,* he thought. It was time for her to go. It was almost eleven, and he wanted to talk to Leila.

"Thank you again," Katrina said for the hundredth time. He didn't want to hear it again. He just wanted her gone. "I promise—"

"Don't worry about it. I just want you to take care of yourself." He held the front door open for her. "I wish you the best of luck," he said.

"You are a lifesaver."

"Take care, Kat," he said and shut the door.

He straightened up the living room and kitchen, then found his cell phone and dialed Leila's number. She answered on the second ring.

"Hey, are you up?" he asked.

"Yes. How are you?"

"Better now to hear your voice," he said.

"Me too, but I'm gonna have to give you a call back, if that's okay. I'm in the middle of something right now."

His heart went south. "Devon," he said, disappointed.

"Yes."

"Okay. Call me back, no matter how late."

"Oh, I will, trust me," she said.

Ray felt a little better. She was thinking about him too. "Okay, bye," he said and hung up.

He went into the kitchen and poured himself a drink. He didn't know what to think or what to do. Was Devon putting the moves on Leila, or was she laying down the law? He was mad at himself for letting Katrina stay so long at his place, because he missed out on seeing Leila. He should have woken her up right after Mia left, let her share her sob story, and gotten her out the damn door, but no, he allowed her to ruin his evening. He looked at the clock, then sat on the sofa and grabbed the remote.

He hoped Leila would call him back soon.

Chapter Seventeen

Leila wondered why Devon didn't understand where she was coming from. They had gone over the same thing five times, and he still didn't accept that she wanted a divorce from him.

"Devon, I tried. I really tried to consider everything you've said. I am not saying that there is no love left in my heart for you. That would be a lie. But there was too much damage done, and I don't want to go back to what we had. Eighty percent of the time, I was miserable."

"I know, Lei. I know that I made bad choices, and I know that I've made horrible mistakes. I wish that I could take it all back, honey. I really wish that I could, but I can't. I just want to make it right. I want to make it up to you. I was an idiot, Lei. Please don't leave now. I know we have what it takes to make it. You just have to try."

"That's the thing. I don't wanna try anymore. I tried for more than two years to make it right, and all you did was toy with me and make threats and criticize me. I allowed you to dictate my days by doing things according to you or trying not to say the wrong thing so you wouldn't walk out the door. I bent over backward trying to please you."

Devon moved closer to her. "And I am willing to bend over backward to please you," he said. He took her hands and held them tight. "I want to do whatever it takes to make this work."

"Devon," she said, looking him in the eyes, "I don't want to hurt you. I don't want to break your heart, baby, because I know how that feels. But I am sorry. What we had is gone. I don't love you the way I did before, and I have grown accustomed to being without you. I don't even see where I fit in your lifestyle. You and I are not the same. I don't want to point fingers, but it is because of you that I am who I am today. I loved you so desperately at one point, but I don't feel like that anymore. Now, please, if you want me to be happy, don't fight me. You know you don't want this."

He had tears in his eyes. "I do. I swear I do."

Her heart ached for him. He seemed so earnest and ready, but that opportunity was gone. She didn't want him anymore. "I know you do, baby," she said and hugged him tightly.

She sat with him for a few moments, and they held hands. She didn't say anything else because there was nothing left to say. He was now the man she had married, the man she remembered falling in love with. The man she had hoped so many nights would return to her. But she had made her decision.

"Devon, please understand that I don't hate you. It is killing me to see you hurt, but don't fight me on this. I will always be here for you, and you will always be in my heart."

"Don't say that. I'm begging you. I don't want this."

"I'm so sorry," she said, sticking to her guns. She couldn't back down. She couldn't let him persuade her to give in to him.

"I won't sign those papers. I know that we are meant to be, and it's just gonna take time for you to realize that." He stood and grabbed his keys to leave.

"Don't do that. Don't fight me. Please don't drag this out. Give me the divorce so we both can move on with our lives."

"But I don't want to move on. I want you."

"Why? Why now?" she yelled.

"Because I love you, Lei. Why is that so hard for you to believe?"

"You've acted like a man who didn't love me for the past two and a half years. You walked out. That's why. You left me when I was pregnant. I had to deal with your lies and your empty promises. You criticized my weight and called me names, and then you packed your things and moved out."

"I never stopped loving you."

"What? You thought you could take a marriage vacation and come back when it was convenient for you and things would be the same?"

"No. I just never thought a day would come when you didn't love me anymore."

"I never thought a day like this would come either, Devon, but it has. I just want a divorce. I want to be free to start over and try new things and be happy."

"We can start over. I know I can make you happy."

"I'm sure you can, but that isn't what I want anymore."

"So, it's really over?"

"I'm afraid so," she said.

"I don't know why it took me this long to realize that I needed to work things out with you, Leila, but now I do. I'm tired of playing bachelor. I want a new start and to leave the single man's life alone." He looked at her for a few seconds and then walked away. He paused at the door before leaving. "I won't fight you, but I will pray that you reconsider your decision before this is final. I hope that we both end up with what we both want."

"Me too," she said.

"I love you. Don't ever forget that."

"I know, and I loved you once too. I'm sorry things had to come to this."

"Yeah, I know. I'll see you in the morning when you drop off the baby."

"Okay. Drive safe," she said.

After he left, she looked at the clock. It was after twelve, but it didn't matter. She wanted to call Ray. She turned everything off, set her alarm, and went upstairs. She stopped in to check on Deja, and to her surprise, she was up.

"Hey, baby girl, what are you doing up?" she asked her baby as she picked her up out of her crib. Her diaper was wet. "Oh, you are soaked. I see why you are up," she said and changed her diaper.

She took Deja into her room with her, propped her up on a pillow, and turned on the television. She put on *Shrek the Third* and turned the volume up a little. It was one of her favorite movies. A few months ago, Deja would watch and say nothing, but she was now making sounds and smiling at the television.

Leila got into bed, grabbed her phone, and dialed Ray's number. He answered on the third ring, and she knew she had woken him up.

"Hey, you," he said when he picked up.

"Hey," she said, smiling.

"I thought I wouldn't hear from you 'til tomorrow."

"Why? I told you I'd call you when I was done."

"How'd it go?"

"Okay, I guess. I'll just have to see how it goes. Devon is pretty upset, but I think he understands that there is nothing left."

"Are you positive that's what you want?"

"Yes, for the hundredth time. I'm sure."

"Okay, if you say so."

"I'm saying so."

"How is your daughter?" he asked.

"She's fine, sitting here wide awake."

"No way. It's after midnight."

"I know, right? But she's right here with her momma, keeping me company."

"I wish I were keeping you company."

"What's stopping you?"

"I don't know, you tell me."

"Well, for one, it's late, and two, it's cold outside."

"I guess that means we have to wait another night."

"I guess. Unless you wanna come over here?"

"Are you serious?" he asked.

"Yeah. I mean, I don't mind you coming over. And I do wanna see you."

She knew it was a bit risky asking him to come over, but Devon didn't live there anymore. And, besides, he allowed Michelle to come over to his place.

"You know what time it is, right?"

"Do you have a curfew?"

"No, but I have a five a.m. client."

"Oh, I'm sorry. I forgot you start early."

"Yes, that is the downside. I'd normally be knocked out at this hour. I get to stay up late on Saturday nights because there are no appointments on Sundays."

"So I guess tomorrow?" she said.

"Sadly, yes," he replied.

"What time will you be done?"

"I had a cancellation for one. Do you think you could break free?"

"Renee and Nicki are both there on Saturdays, so I can sneak away for a little while."

"Cool."

"Tomorrow at one, right?"

"Yes, ma'am."

"Well, I'll be sure to be there."

"I'm happy to hear that."

"I'll let you go so you can get some sleep and be well rested for me."

"Oh, trust, I'll be rested," he said, yawning again.

"I gotcha. Good night," she said, and they hung up.

She didn't have to get up as early as he did, and she had to figure out how she was going to get her baby to sleep. "DJ, it's time for you to go to bed, baby," she said, taking her into her nursery.

"Dada, dada," Deja said, reaching over Leila's shoulder as if she were looking for Devon.

"Daddy isn't here, sweet pea," she said, trying to put her down in her crib. Deja began to kick and scream. Leila was surprised to see her behave that way.

"Dada, dada," Deja cried, reaching her hands and kicking her little chunky legs.

"Deja, what's wrong, baby? Your daddy isn't here," she said, picking her up.

Deja cried and rubbed her sleepy eyes. That made Leila want to call Devon to come back over, but she quickly decided against it.

"Hell naw. I'm not calling him. You are going have to cut it out, sweet pea, and go your little behind to sleep."

She took Deja back to her room and got in the bed with her. After the baby fussed for a little while, she stopped crying and went to sleep. Leila took her back to her crib and realized that Deja knew who Devon was. Maybe it was a bad idea to take her around Ray. She didn't want to confuse her by bringing another man into her life.

She climbed back into her bed and smiled. She was going to see him and get some more of his good loving. He had what it took to make her weak. Her last thoughts before she drifted off to sleep were about how sexy his back was when he was standing in front of his armoire.

Chapter Eighteen

"Okay, I'll see you next week," Ray said to his client as he opened the door to let him out.

Leila was standing there, getting ready to knock. When he saw her, his man jumped in his pants. He had been counting the minutes, anticipating the moment he could kiss her again. As soon as he shut the door, he grabbed her and kissed her lips and then gave her a soft kiss on the forehead.

"Hello to you too," she said, smiling.

"Hey," he said and returned the smile.

"I see someone is happy to see me."

"I can't tell you how anxious I was. And I don't wanna waste too much time standing out here talking."

He pulled her closer to him, and they kissed again. They broke apart long enough for her to follow him into his bedroom. There, he started undressing her, kissing her neck and her shoulders. He turned her away from him and kissed her back. Leila closed her eyes and enjoyed the feel of his warm breath caressing her skin. He made it a point not to miss a spot as he kissed her down her back and slid her panties down. He kissed her on the back of her thighs, and she let out a deep breath.

He wrapped his arms around her waist and kissed her ass cheeks, then slowly moved back up to her neck. Leila moaned, and the sound of her heavy breathing let him know that he was on the right track. He sucked on the side of her neck and massaged her breasts from behind. She closed her eyes, and he imagined she enjoyed the warm kisses he planted on her skin.

Her breasts began to leak milk. "I'm sorry," she said, looking embarrassed when she saw it running down his forearm.

He turned her to face him and kissed her. "You don't have to apologize, Leila. This is a natural thing."

"I know, but it is so not sexy," she said, and they laughed.

"It's a little different from what I'm used to, but I'm okay," he said. He went into the bathroom and brought back a towel. He wiped his hands and arms and handed the towel to Leila so she could wipe her stomach.

"Thanks," she said after dabbing her nipples. She handed him the towel back.

"This is not a big deal. I'll just have to be gentle," he said and kissed her left breast softly. "And I will try to resist the urge to suck on them."

"You think you can resist? Because I wish you could suck on them."

"I know, but these belong to Deja right now, so that means I won't get to pleasure these the way I wanna 'til a little later on down the line."

He was talking like they had a future together. She smiled. "Later on down the line, huh?"

"Yeah, if you allow me to be around you for a while."

"How do you know that you will want to be around me for a while?" she asked as he kissed her neck.

"So far, I feel like this is gonna go far, but you and I just will have to see, won't we?" he said, pulling her closer.

They moved over to his bed, and she lay down on her back. Ray kissed and licked her nipples, then moved down her body. She closed her eyes as his tongue traveled over her body.

"Aw, baby, please don't do that," she moaned.

"You want me to stop?" he asked. He knew she didn't. He was licking her spot, and her body quivered.

"No, I don't want you to stop," she said between deep breaths and pants. "Oh, baby. Oooh, that's good. Aw . . . aw, baby, that feels so good," she said.

He felt her body jerk against his mouth. "Damn, you came already?"

"Yes, yes, and I can't believe it." She covered her face with the covers.

He smiled at her obvious embarrassment. "Wow, a new record for me," he said and kissed her inner thigh.

"It's been so long since I've had that done to me. Your tongue is like magic," she said.

Ray pulled the covers from her face to look at her. "You liked that?" he asked, climbing on top of her.

"Oh, yes, I did like that, baby," she said and kissed him.

She rubbed his back, and they rolled over. She kissed his chest and rubbed his erection through his shorts. She wanted to do to him what he had just finished doing to her, so she pulled his shorts and boxers off. He relaxed and allowed her to take his man inside of her mouth. The warmth and wetness of her mouth made him moan. She knew what she was doing. The thought made him more excited. It didn't take long before he was ready to burst.

"Leila, baby. Yes, yes, baby," he moaned. He rubbed the back of her head and concentrated hard so he wouldn't explode in her mouth. "Oh, yeah. Ooh, shit, baby," he said. He was close to losing it. He hadn't had good head in a long time, and Leila was giving a superstar performance. "Baby, stop. No, baby, stop. I'm gon' bust. Please," he said, trying to pull her off. She sat up and smiled at him. "Damn, girl, you get down like that?" he asked.

"I aim to please," she boasted. "You like that?" she asked, rubbing her fingertips over his erection.

"Come here," he said, grabbing her face and kissing her passionately.

He rolled to the side, reached across to his nightstand drawer, and got a condom. Leila watched him rip it open and put it on. He leaned in and kissed her again before he pushed himself inside of her. After a few strokes, he pushed her legs back farther, making sure he got as deep as he could. Her tunnel was soaking wet, and he could hear her juices pop as he slid in and out of her. It was even better than it was the first time.

Ray closed his eyes. "Oh, baby, you feel good," he said, He was enjoying every stroke, and it sounded like she was too. "Leila, baby," he moaned.

He leaned down and thrust his tongue into her mouth, mimicking the movement of his manhood into her wetness. She felt so good. He sucked her chin and licked her neck. He wanted to eat her up. They used their entire hour going at it, working up a sweat. He was behind her in mid-stroke on their second round when his next appointment knocked at the door.

"Damn, what time is it?" Ray asked, still holding her hips and pumping.

"I think I heard the door," Leila said, not answering his question. She was on her knees facing the window and couldn't see the clock.

"I know, but it's right there," he said, still pumping. There was another knock, and he moved faster. "Oh, damn," he said when he came. He steadied himself so he wouldn't collapse onto Leila. They were sweaty, and he smelled like sex. The whole room did. He needed a shower before going near his client.

"Baby, the door," she said again.

He pulled out of her. "I know, I know. I hear it." He went into the bathroom and came back with a robe. "Here, put this on, and tell Nina to give me ten minutes."

Leila looked at him. "You want me to go out there looking like this?"

"I gotta shower," he said. She shook her head but got up and put the robe on. "Thanks," he said and ran to get into the shower.

When he came out ten minutes later, she was sitting on the side of the bed. "How'd it go? Is Nina upstairs?"

"Oh, yeah, she's up there all right," Leila said and got under the covers.

"What does that mean?"

"She told me to tell you to hurry up because she is a paying customer. Like I'm not."

"She didn't mean it like that," he said, stepping into his boxers.

Leila sighed. "Yeah, whatever."

"Don't pay them any attention, okay?" He wished she wouldn't let his female clients get to her.

"Easy for you to say. Christa looks at me like I'm shit, and Nina just looked at me like I am a fat monster. I wonder what the rest of them will think after they find out that you and I are seeing each other. When they all find out that Ray chose the fat one," she groused.

"You are not fat, and I don't care what they think. And neither should you. Eventually, they'll all know. I'm happy with the choice I made, so fuck 'em," he said. "Now, how long do you have? I've got to head upstairs," he said, pulling his tank top over his head.

"I'm good. I'll hang out here for a while."

"Okay. You can shower if you want. Towels are in the linen closet. Help yourself to the fridge and make yourself at home." He leaned in to kiss her. "Be done soon, okay?"

"Yeah, babe, I'm cool. Go on," she said with a weak smile.

Leila wondered why women acted so evil toward one another. Why was she getting the dirty looks and the frowns? She was just as beautiful as the next woman, and her size-twelve body was fine with her and Ray, so she didn't understand.

She got up and went into the living room to get the bag she brought with her. She had remembered to bring her blow dryer and curling irons this time. She wanted to make sure she looked better than she did the last time she was there. She showered and did her hair, putting a few curls in it. She put on a little makeup, even though she still glowed from her lovemaking with Ray. She went to the kitchen to grab a bottle of water and overheard Nina and Ray talking upstairs.

"Are you fucking her?" she heard Nina ask.

"Excuse me? Where do you get off asking me about my personal business?" he asked.

"Christa was right?"

"Christa is going around telling my business?"

"Well, Ray, we're just all wondering how our flirting and trying to hook up with you hasn't worked, and as soon as Big Momma start coming, you decide to just hook up with her."

Leila gasped and put a hand to her chest. *Who the hell does she think she is? She's about to get a Big-Momma beatdown.*

Nina was still talking. "Now I understand you not wanting to hook up with Christa and some of them other hoes, but over me? What's up with you?"

"Nina, your session is over, and you need to keep your opinions about Leila and my other clients to yourself. You need to remember that we have a business relationship, and I don't have to explain to you who I choose to see or date or why I chose them. You and your little chatty friends are starting to wear me out. If you'd like to keep coming and continue doing business with me, I'd advise you to keep your nose out of my personal affairs."

"Okay, Ray, damn. I gotcha. Just tell me this, what does she have that I don't?"

"My darling, you are a beautiful woman, and any man who can see wouldn't look past you. But to keep our relationship professional, my answer to that question is simply nothing."

"Nothing?"

Leila could hear the confusion in Nina's voice.

"Okay," Ray said. Leila heard his impatience in his voice. "Nina, you are gorgeous, yes. Listen to me. I am attracted to women. I am just as attracted to Leila as I would be to you. She is just as beautiful, funny, and sweet as you are, in my opinion." There was no answer from Nina. "I gotta get ready for my next client," he said. "Will I see you for your next session?"

It sounded like Nina clicked her tongue. "Of course I'll be back," she said. "I can't just hand my body over to another trainer."

Leila heard her coming downstairs. She was sitting on the sofa, drinking her water by the time the other woman got to the bottom step.

"Leila," she said. She looked disappointed.

Leila stifled the urge to curse. "Nina," she said instead and got up to follow her to the door.

"Look, Leila, my apologies for earlier. You, my sista, are lucky. This one is definitely not an easy win," she said, pointing upstairs where Ray was.

"I've heard," Leila said. She agreed. Rayshon was unique, a gift she planned to cherish.

"Yeah, and he's a good guy. Good luck to ya, because I know at least sixty percent of his female clients are gonna be pissed. And they are not a nice crowd."

"Thanks for the heads-up," she said and smiled.

"It was nice to meet you. I guess I'll be seeing you around."

"Nice to have met you too." Leila held the door open for Nina to leave and shut it behind her. *I guess she's not all bitch.*

"Hey," Ray said, coming up behind her.

"Hey," she said.

He pulled her close and kissed her. "I'm sorry about that. A lot of my female clients have tried to hook up, so there's going to be a lot of upset women for the next few weeks 'til they get used to you."

"I see," she said, putting her head down.

"Please don't let them get to you. I'm with you because I wanna be, okay?" He lifted her chin. "Just ignore their asses. Fuck their attitudes, snide remarks, and negativity."

"Are you sure I'm what you want? I'm not worried about them. I'm a grown-ass woman, and I couldn't care less about what them bitches think or say about me or if they think I'm a Big Momma. I just wanna make sure you're okay with it."

"I'm perfectly fine," he said and smiled. She smiled back and was about to kiss him when there was a knock at the door. "That's Samara," he said.

"Should I get that?" she asked.

"Yeah, you should, and make sure you introduce yourself," he said and headed for the steps.

Leila turned, took a deep breath, and opened the door to another gorgeous woman. She shook her head. *This is only the beginning.*

Chapter Nineteen

"Devon, I need to go," Leila said into the phone. "You said you'd watch DJ this weekend. You can't back out at the last minute."

"I'm not backing out. I'm asking you where you're going."

"And I'm telling you again, none of your business," she said, irritated.

"If you can't tell me where you're going, I can't keep her."

"You can't look after your own child?" she barked.

Their divorce hadn't been finalized yet. They were in a six-month reconciliation period ordered by the court because he had told the judge he wanted a chance to reconcile. She had wanted to punch him in his face when they left the courtroom, and she wanted to do it again now. She had made plans to have the weekend off so she could be with Ray.

"Leila, why can't you just say where you are going?"

"You know what? Forget it, okay? You don't have to keep DJ. I'll figure something out," she said and slammed the phone down. She wasn't going to beg him for anything. She wanted to cry. She just wanted to have a weekend not worrying about the baby. She was spending the weekend at Ray's, and his place wasn't baby friendly.

Twenty minutes later, she sat listening to the phone ring, ignoring Devon's back-to-back calls. She didn't have anything to say to him and didn't want to hear his irritating-ass voice. She had called Renee to see if she could keep the baby for her, but since they had planned to close the store that Saturday three weeks ago, she and her husband had plans.

Leila fought the tears as she tried to figure out how to tell Ray. She really didn't want to cancel, but she had no choice. She had no one else she could trust to keep her little one. She didn't want to tell him that she couldn't make it, but she was left with no choice. She took a deep breath and dialed his number. She looked over at her little angel and realized she was making the right decision. Her little girl was more important. Her heart pounded as she waited for him to pick up.

"Hey, beautiful," he said. She could hear his smile in his voice.

"What's up?" she said nervously. She didn't want to back out of their romantic weekend, but she had no choice.

"Nothing too much, just finishing up dinner," he said. She heard kitchen noises in the background.

"Um, listen," she said, biting her bottom lip, "I'm not going to be able to make it. Devon is being a jerk. I am afraid I'm going to have to cancel our weekend."

"What? Are you serious? You can't be serious," he said. "What happened?" He sounded angry. "Baby, I reorganized my whole schedule to free up this weekend, so I can't be hearing you can't make it."

"I'm sorry, but Devon is tripping. He says he can't take the baby this weekend. I didn't want to call you and cancel, but I don't have a sitter for Deja." She struggled not to cry.

"Just bring her with you," he said.

Bringing her wasn't a good idea. "I can't, Ray. Deja is walking now and into everything, and your place isn't baby safe. It's not Deja friendly. And where would she sleep?"

"She can't get hurt over here, and she can sleep with us."

"I'd enjoy myself, but there are no toys, and you have hardwood floors and sharp end tables. My baby would be miserable."

He sighed, and she could feel his disappointment through the phone line. "We can get a hotel suite with carpet or something. Just please tell me that we are still on for this weekend," he pleaded. "I cooked dinner for you, and I have chilled wine and a bubble bath and candles. I rearranged my entire work week for this weekend. You can't say no."

"Baby, I know, and I'm so sorry." They both went silent and then it hit her. "Why don't you come over here for the weekend?"

"I don't think that's a good idea."

"Why not? Devon and I are done, and this is where I live. He entertains and has guests at his condo, so why can't I?"

"Your name ain't on his condo. Technically, that's still his house you live in."

"Well, technically, he doesn't get his mail here and hasn't lived here since I was three months pregnant with my ten-month-old. So he doesn't live here," she snapped.

"I would love to come, and trust me when I say I do want to see you this weekend, but I wouldn't feel comfortable in his house."

"Then I guess I'll see you next week sometime," she said, disappointed.

"Hold on. It's like that?"

"Like what? I invited you to my home to spend the weekend with me, and you said no. What else is left to say?" she asked, taking off her earrings. She had gotten her hair and makeup done and bought a new outfit, and it was all for nothing.

"I guess you're right." He sighed again. "Can you at least come to have dinner with me?"

"Yeah, I can do that," she said, smiling. There was hope. At least she could see him for a few hours.

"Thank you," he said. He sounded relieved.

"No, thank you. Just understand I've got to bring Deja," she said.

"That's cool. I hope she likes lamb," he joked.

"Naw, but her mommy does," Leila said, putting her earrings back on.

"I'll see you ladies soon."

"We are on our way."

It was so cold, so she bundled both of them up and headed for the door. Devon called again, and she hit the button to ignore the call. She wished he'd get the hint and stop calling. By the time she made it to Ray's, Deja was asleep. She called him, and he came down to help her. When they got upstairs, he took the baby into his room. Leila followed him and took off her coat, hat, and sweater.

"She is getting so big," he commented. "And she is beautiful."

"Thanks. This li'l piggy gets into everything." She said and placed Deja in the middle of the bed. The platform bed was low, and Deja knew how to get off the couch, so she figured she'd be fine.

They left the baby asleep in the bed and went to the kitchen. Leila watched Ray get glasses and plates for them.

"The food smells divine," she said, taking in the aroma.

"Thanks. I hope you enjoy it," he said, handing her a glass. "Have a seat."

Leila sat at the small dinner table he had in a corner off the kitchen. Candles burned and soft music played. He joined her, and they ate and talked and laughed.

"Why do you always have red wine?" she asked when he refilled her glass. Red was fine, but white was more her flavor.

"Well, my dear, red wines are better for your heart, and they don't have all the calories that are in white wines. Plus, red goes well with beef, red sauces, and lamb." He got up to clear the table.

"I got you, but white wine tastes better to me," she commented as she got up to help him.

Besides, he exercised all the time, so the extra calories wouldn't affect his physique at all.

They cleaned the kitchen together and settled in the living room. He pulled one of her feet onto his lap and started massaging it. She closed her eyes and enjoyed it. Just when he took her other foot, they heard a loud thump and then her baby screaming. Leila launched herself from the sofa, and Ray was right behind her. Leila examined Deja and saw that she was more frightened than hurt.

"I'm sorry. I had no idea my bed would be too high," Ray said.

"It's not your fault. She just woke up in a strange place, that's all. The fall scared her. She isn't hurt."

Ray went into the bathroom and brought back a cold towel. "I know, but I hate that she fell," he said.

"She's fine," Leila said. Deja was no longer crying. She was looking around, trying to figure out where she was.

"I know, but—"

Leila interrupted him. "Babe, look. She's okay."

They went back to the living room and took Deja with them. Leila sat on the couch, and the baby wanted to get down, so she let her go. She saw Ray watching Deja. He looked nervous.

"Listen," he said, "I wanna be with you this weekend, so if it would be better for your daughter if we went to your place, I'd like to go."

Leila smiled. "Really?"

"Yes, really," he said and kissed her. "Let me grab a few things and then we can go."

He went into his room, packed a few things, and then they all got bundled up and left. They decided it was better for him to follow her so she would not have to bring him back on Sunday.

Chapter Twenty

"Come on in," Leila told Ray as he followed her into the entryway of her three-level brick home.

It was beautifully decorated, he thought as he looked around. "Wow, Leila. Your home is amazing."

She took his coat and hung it in the coat closet. "Thanks. Give me a moment and I'll show you around," she said.

She unbundled Deja and put her down. The baby immediately headed for the stairs and began to climb them.

"She's climbing the stairs," Ray said, not believing his eyes.

"It's cool," she said. "She's just going up to her room. I used to be nervous when she went for the stairs, but after a couple weeks of trying to stop her, I gave in and allowed her to explore. I was also surprised when I saw her little body climb all twelve steps and go into her own room. She has the stairs down to a science. Come, let me show you the rest of the place."

Ray followed Leila. They started on the main floor, and she showed him her huge gourmet kitchen and spacious family room. He peeped into the two spare bedrooms and admired her formal living and dining room. They headed downstairs into the basement, and Ray thought he had walked into heaven when he laid eyes on the finished home theater. He was floored when she told him that she didn't go down there at all.

She showed him the small office area and spare bathroom, and then they headed up to the third level. They stopped to check on Deja. She was so busy entertaining herself that she didn't notice them.

After they took a quick look at the hall bathroom, Leila showed him to her master suite, telling him this was where they would be retiring for the night. Ray grinned at her. They went back down to the kitchen, and she grabbed a bottle of white wine from her wine cooler.

"White, huh?" he said and made himself comfortable at the island.

"Yep. I told you I love it," she said and grabbed a couple of glasses from the cabinet.

"Did you do all of the decorating?" he asked.

She handed him a glass of wine. "Everything except for the basement. That was all Devon's doing. And then he bounced," she said and laughed a little.

"That must have been hard. Is that why you don't go down there?"

"No. I'm mostly here by myself with the baby." She shrugged. "We don't need HD and surround sound to watch *Shrek*," she said.

Ray laughed. "I don't know now. A huge flat-screen HD set like that would make Esther from *Sanford and Son* look like 'America's Next Top Model,'" he said.

This time, Leila laughed. "I wouldn't know. I've never turned it on."

"Get out," he said, shocked. "You're joking, right?"

"Nope. Devon watched it a few times with his pals, and not too long after the construction was done, he was done with me." She looked away.

"Let's go sit on the sofa," Ray said, taking her hand. They sat in silence for a few moments before he spoke again. "I'm so looking forward to getting married and buying a home as beautiful as this one and having a couple kids."

Leila's brows went up. "Really? I'm surprised. You actually want to get married?"

"Oh, yeah," he said and took a swallow of his wine.

"Wow. The idea of me ever being married again is, like, nonexistent."

"Why would you say that?"

"Because I'm not getting any younger, I have a kid, and I don't exactly look like 'America's Next Top Model.'"

"Please, Leila, don't even. You know you are beautiful, and there is nothing wrong with the fact that you already have a child. You never know what's in store for your future."

"I guess you're right. I just don't want to marry the wrong man again, you know?" She shook her head. "Devon and I were inseparable once, and now it's like I can't remember how good it was when it was good."

"That's all behind you. You have to look at what's good in front of you. I'm here with you, and I want to make memories with you that you will never have trouble remembering."

Leila was about to speak when she felt movement by her leg. She looked down and saw Deja. "Hey, sweet pea, what's up?" she asked the baby.

"Ba, ba, ba," Deja said.

"Bottle? You want your bottle?" Leila asked.

"Ba, ba," Deja said again.

Ray followed them into the kitchen and watched as Leila prepared a bottle. They went back into the living room, and she put Deja on the sofa and ran up to get her nightclothes. When she came back, she put a fresh diaper on the baby, got her into her bedclothes, and gave her the bottle. She was asleep before she was even halfway done with her bottle. Ray followed Leila when she took her upstairs to her nursery. They left the door partially open and went back down to the kitchen, where Ray refilled their glasses.

"I could have gotten it for you," she said, taking the glass he handed her.

"No, baby, it's cool," he said and followed her back into the family room.

Leila grabbed the remote and turned on some soft music. They sat and talked a little but mostly just looked at one another. They finished their wine and decided to head up to bed. Ray grabbed his bag, and Leila made sure the door was locked and set the alarm. When they got upstairs, she went into the bathroom and started the water so she could take a bath.

"The remote is here," she told Ray and handed it to him. "I'm not sure what you wanna watch, but knock yourself out."

"I wanna watch you," he said.

The hairs on the back of her neck stood up. "Watch me what?" she asked.

"Take a bath," he said, moving close to her.

"Really?" she asked.

"Yes, really," he said and tossed the remote onto the bed.

Ray took her by the hand, led her into the master bath, and started to undress her. She stepped into the tub while the water was still running and lay back to make herself comfortable. He put his hand in the water and began to rub her legs, making his way up and past her inner thighs and up to her breasts. She closed her eyes and enjoyed his caress.

He reached over and turned the faucet off. "You are a lovely woman, Leila, inside and out. You have so many qualities beyond your outer beauty, and I wouldn't change one thing about you," he said.

Leila blushed. "I honestly couldn't wait 'til the bubbles rose and covered my ugly stretch marks," she confessed.

"I'll be right back." Ray stood and walked out. He came back a moment later. "Here we go," he said, lighting the candles she had sitting around her tub and on her vanity. He turned out the lights and returned to her side.

"This is nice," she said, giving him a smile.

"Yes, it is," he said, taking one of her hands out of the water and kissing her fingers.

"You are so perfect. Sometimes it amazes me how sweet and kind you are to me. I mean, I would never try to compete with any other woman, but a few weeks ago, when we first hooked up, I didn't take you as seriously as I do now. I keep telling myself that any moment now, a camera crew is gonna come out of the woodwork saying, 'Aha, gotcha.'"

"I understand what you're saying, and you know, it is a shame, or should I say, it's sad for anybody to ever think they aren't good enough or fine enough or sexy enough for someone. I mean, I know that people are attracted to beauty, but when I decided to go into physical fitness a few years ago, I learned early that beauty comes in all shapes, sizes, and attitudes.

"I have worked with women who you couldn't get with even if you look like Morris Chestnut or Denzel Washington. They were interested in men with money, and looks have absolutely nothing to do with it. I've met some who are not so fine or eye-catching according to society's standards, but they're so confident in who they are that no one could convince them that they weren't as fine as Halle Berry or Nia Long. I'm sorry you felt like me wanting you was a joke or some kind of game. From now on, please, for me, know that I am not all that and nothing or no one is too good for you."

"Devon used to call me names and tell me that I wasn't going anywhere with him looking like a cow. When I was pregnant, I remember him comparing me to the Goodyear Blimp. That stuck out in my mind, and I heard it every time you'd ever say I was beautiful. Ray, you've shown me nothing but kindness. I was the one with the hang-ups because Devon had my mind messed up. He had me convinced that I wasn't attractive anymore and that no one would ever want me again."

"He is an idiot."

"So, I can relax?"

He chuckled. "Yes, baby, I want you to relax," he whispered.

He went back to exploring her body. He touched, rubbed, and massaged every inch that he had access to. He moved his focus to her clit and rubbed it until she moaned out loud and gasped for air.

"Oh, my goodness," she whispered, trying to catch her breath.

Ray sat back on his haunches and grinned at her. "You liked that, baby?"

"You know I liked that. You know I did," she said.

He stood up, undid his belt, and took off his shirt, then went into her room. When he came back, he had his toiletry bag in hand.

She closed her eyes for a moment, still trying to regain her composure. When she opened them again, he was naked. She watched as he opened the shower door, turned on the water, and waited for it to warm up before he stepped in. She leaned back in the tub and enjoyed the view as he lathered up. He was so sexy and fine. And he wanted to be with her.

He grabbed the bottle of soap again to lather once more, and she felt throbbing between her legs when he lathered up his dick. She slid a hand into the water and touched herself. Watching him stroke himself, she came again. *I'm in trouble.*

She sat up and grabbed her Bath & Body Works bath gel, finished her bath, and got out of the tub. She grabbed her robe and found one of Devon's that he hadn't taken with him for Ray to use. He was drying off when she walked back into the bathroom.

"What's that for?" he asked, looking at the robe in her hand.

"It's for you. It's a robe," she said.

"I don't need that," he said. "And you don't need this one either." He grabbed the belt of her robe and used it to pull her to him.

He grabbed her face and kissed her, pushing her robe off her shoulders and letting it drop to the floor. He ran his tongue down her neck and went for a nipple. The sucking sensation made her moan out loud, and she felt the heat between her legs.

Ray took her into his strong arms and sat her on the vanity between the two sinks. He used his fingers to test her wetness, then he went down and began to lick her. She gasped and moaned as he used his tongue to please her. She grabbed the back of his head and held it, breathlessly telling him how good it felt. Before she knew it, she was coming again. She couldn't remember ever in her life having three orgasms in less than an hour, or even three in one day, as a matter of fact.

"Baby, please," she begged. "Please, no more. I'm gonna pass out."

"Naw, I'm not done with you yet," he said.

Leila felt her legs get weak. "Give me a minute. I promise I'm going to let you have your way with me. I just need a minute to recuperate, and I need to look in on Deja." She needed to get away from him for a few minutes. He was doing the unthinkable to her, and she was falling in love before her divorce was final.

"Okay, but hurry back." He planted a wet kiss on her lips.

"I will," she said and inched away from him.

She walked out into the hall naked and peeped on her sleeping baby. She had known Deja would be sound asleep, but she had to get her second wind. She turned around and went back to her bedroom.

Ray was waiting in her bed. "Come here, sexy, so I can get some of that good stuff you got," he said, pulling back the covers.

She laughed. "You are too much," she said as she climbed into bed.

"Aw, you ain't seen anything yet," he said and gave her the best of the best lovemaking she had ever had. After coming for the fourth time, she collapsed on his chest. The last thing she remembered before going to sleep was the kiss he put on her forehead.

The next morning, Deja was up at seven. Leila dragged herself out of bed and went downstairs to get her a bottle. She tried to get her back to sleep, but she was up and talking and wanting to get out of her crib.

Leila sighed and went to the hall bathroom to relieve her bladder, then went back into her room and slipped on some sweats and a halter. She and the baby headed downstairs, and Leila cooked her some eggs and grits. Deja ate, and the two of them watched television and played for a while. Before she knew it, it was afternoon. Ray was still sleeping, and she didn't bother to wake him. By one, Deja began to get restless and was ready for a nap. Leila got her down and decided she was going to make herself something to eat.

Chapter Twenty-one

Leila turned on some music, made herself a mimosa, and took out the items she needed for an omelet. Despite the time, she had decided to make breakfast food. She put a few strips of bacon on a pan and put it in the oven and sang along with the music as she diced vegetables for the omelet.

Ray walked into the kitchen, wearing shorts and a tank. "Good morning, beautiful," he said. When he kissed her, she smelled the fresh scent of Crest on his breath.

"Good afternoon, handsome," she said and pointed at the digital readout on her microwave.

"Damn, girl, you put a brother out," he said. He took a sip of her mimosa and frowned. "What's this?" he asked.

"It's a mimosa," she said and took her glass out of his hand.

"That's what they taste like?" He took the glass back and tried it again.

"You've never had a mimosa?" she asked, turning on a burner on the stove.

"I've wanted to but never have." He opened the cabinet to get a glass.

"Well, I love them. Do you want me to make you one?"

"Sure. Do you need help with anything?"

"No, just have a seat and let me cook for you for a change," she said. She always went to his loft, so he did most of the cooking.

"Where's Deja?"

"Oh, she's napping. That girl got up at seven this morning." After making him his drink, she cracked eggs and poured them in a pan.

"No way," he said. He sat down at the island and sipped the mimosa.

"Yes way." She watched the eggs start to set, hoping she turned out a perfect omelet for Ray. She took the bacon out of the stove and dropped the lever on the four-slice toaster to toast bagels for the both of them.

"Wow, baby, you've been up since seven?" he asked.

"Yeah, but I'm good," she said and flipped a perfect omelet. She added the veggies and shredded cheese, then grabbed the whisk to get her own eggs ready to go into the skillet. The toaster popped up as she poured her eggs into the frying pan, and she took two bagel halves out and put them on Ray's plate with his omelet and bacon. She put his plate in front of him, set out fresh strawberries and cantaloupe she had cut up earlier, and went back to flip her omelet. It was perfect too. She grabbed the cream cheese from the fridge and gave him a butter knife.

"No thanks, babe," he said.

"What do you mean? Strawberry cream cheese is the bomb." She slid her omelet onto a plate and turned off the fire.

"I know, but it's loaded with tons of fat and calories, and it's not good for you."

Leila paused. "I don't see a little cream cheese blowing away your six pack."

"I know that, and I'm not suggesting that you not enjoy your cream cheese. I just don't touch the stuff." He pushed it toward her, but she didn't touch it. She pushed her plate forward and grabbed her glass. This was turning into Devon all over again.

"What's wrong?" he asked.

"I don't feel like eating anymore," she said and turned away.

"Why? What did I do?" he asked.

"Nothing, at least not yet," she said. She heard her voice crack.

"What? I'm lost. What just happened?"

"You think I'm a pig because I like cream cheese?" she asked.

"Whoa, baby. What are you talking about? I don't think that. Why would you ask me something like that?"

"Devon used to do that, make a remark about food that I like, as if I weren't supposed to eat." She blinked to keep tears from falling.

"I don't have a problem with you loving cream cheese. If you wanna load up your bagel, go right ahead. You wanting to have cream cheese on your bagel does not make you a pig. I am not trying to change you or make you do what I do. If you want the cream cheese, knock yourself out. And," he said, holding up one finger, "I am not Devon. I know how he ruined your self-esteem and criticized you every chance he had, and I'm sorry you had to experience that. But please recognize that I am Rayshon Johnson, and I would never think something so horrible about my lady.

"You are who I chose. To choose you and then think ill shit like that is not who I am. Please eat your food and pack on all the cream cheese you want." He caressed her cheek. "I am completely happy with you the way you are."

Now Leila felt a little foolish. Ray hadn't done anything to make her compare him with trifling-ass Devon. She put a load of cream cheese on her bagel and sat down with Ray to enjoy her food.

After eating, they went into the family room to watch a little TV. They had just gotten comfortable on the sofa when Deja woke up, ready for lunch.

Leila was drained, but she went into mommy mode. She took out macaroni and cheese and heated it up, then took Deja into the family room. She yawned and sat back down next to Ray.

"Listen, baby," he said, "let me take her and feed her. You go up and get a nap."

"No, I'm good," she said and yawned again.

"You're exhausted," he insisted. "I can feed and take care of Deja."

"You don't know how to take care of her," she protested.

"How hard can it be?" he asked, taking Deja from her lap and grabbing the bowl.

When Deja didn't cry, Leila relaxed a little. "I am sleepy," she confessed.

"I know, so go upstairs and rest. Me and Deja gon' eat our mac and cheese and hang out."

"Are you sure, Ray?" she asked, still a little skeptical.

"Go. I got this," he said.

Leila went upstairs and was asleep before her head hit the pillow. When she woke up, three hours had passed. She couldn't believe she had slept that long. She went to the bathroom and then went downstairs. Ray and Deja weren't in the family room. A pang of fear sliced through her, and she hoped he hadn't left the house with her baby. She walked over and looked out the window. His truck was still there. She called his name but didn't get an answer. The only other place they could be was the basement.

She opened the basement door and heard the television. She started walking down the steps and heard Deja laughing. And not just her usual laugh. She was laughing hard and loud. When she got to the bottom, she saw Ray carrying Deja around in the air like she was an airplane. The baby was cracking up.

"Hey, you two," she said.

"Look," Ray said, "there's Mommy." Deja kept laughing.

"Come here, you," Leila said, taking Deja and kissing her on the cheek. "Are you having fun?" She looked at Ray. "How was she?"

"She was good." He reached over and tickled Deja. "We've been having a ball."

"Why did you come down here?"

"Because this is a cool space. I noticed the PS3, so Deja and I played a little boxing and a little football. We've just been hanging out down here. I hope you don't mind."

"No, not at all. I had no idea that thing was even still here, as a matter of fact."

He gestured to the audiovisual setup. "You mean to tell me you really don't come down here to enjoy any of this?" he asked again.

"No, I don't. Really."

"You got a big-ass flat screen and these comfy leather recliners, and you don't watch movies down here?"

"Why is that so hard to believe?"

"Because this setup is so great. Tonight, my dear, your days of not coming down here and enjoying this home theater are over. We are going to order pizza and get popcorn, candy, and stuff I know I'm gonna regret eating tomorrow, and we are going to watch movies. If I had a room like this, I'd only come out for work," he said.

Leila looked around and wondered why she hadn't enjoyed the space before. It really was a travesty that she was letting it go to waste.

She smiled. "Okay, but we need to head to the video store because I don't have any recent movies."

The three of them put on their coats, got in her truck, and headed to the video store. Since it was cold, Leila and Deja stayed in the truck while Ray went inside to get the movies. Leila's phone rang, and she dug around her purse to get it. Her good mood faded when she saw that it was Devon.

"Hello," she answered, irritated.

"Leila, what in the hell is going on with you?" he yelled.

"What is it? What do you want?" She was in no mood for his ass, and she wished she hadn't answered the phone.

"I called you all damn night and been calling you all day, and your phone kept going straight to voicemail. And your cell phone, you just don't bother to answer it?"

"Why didn't you use your brain and figure out I didn't want to talk to you?" She saw Ray coming out of the store.

"Don't play with me. As long as my child is with you, you need to answer your phone."

"Deja is fine, okay? If she weren't, I would have called you. Why are you so concerned now, when you could have had your child this entire weekend?" She held up one finger when Ray opened the door. She didn't want him to say anything.

"I would have taken care of her if you had just told me where you were going."

"That's not your business. So what is it you want now?"

"I want to come and see Deja."

Leila rolled her eyes. "Please don't call me with this 'I wanna see my baby' crap."

"You're starting to piss me off, you know that?"

"Oh well. And I'm not home, anyway."

"Where are you?"

"Not home," she spat.

"Not home where?" he yelled. "Where in the hell are you with my child?"

"You need to calm down and lower your voice. My daughter is with me, and she is fine."

"And I want to see her, so where are you?"

"You can see her, Devon, but it won't be to-night," she told him.

"Like hell it won't," he yelled.

"Look, did you want anything important?"

"Yes, I want you to bring your ass home and let me see my child."

"No," she said. Ray touched her hand, and she looked at him. She saw concern in his eyes. She motioned for him to drive. "You don't control me, and I'm not going to let you tell me what to do," she said into the phone. "I'm not going to cancel or change my plans to accommo-date your ass. You will see DJ tomorrow."

"You know what, Lei? I will see you at the house."

There would definitely be a scene if he came to her house and saw her with Ray. "Well, you can wait all night because I won't be home 'til tomorrow," she said, lying.

"Don't fucking play with me. Bring yo' ass home," he yelled. "And who the fuck does this Tahoe belong to in our driveway?"

He's at my house? "Our driveway? You mean my driveway. You live at 2240 Park Avenue, not 404 Langston Place," she said.

"Lei . . ."

She heard a warning in his tone, and she got even more pissed. "No, no, no, Devon. Here's where reality kicks in and hits you in the face. We are no more. I am not with you, and you and I do not live together. You moved on when you moved out, and now I am moving on. M-o-v-i-n-g on," she said, spelling it out. "So get your ass away from my house, and I will see you tomorrow." She hit the button to end the call and leaned her head back against the headrest. Her phone rang again. It was Devon again. She hit IGNORE, and it rang again seconds later. She hit IGNORE again, and he called right back.

"Baby, you should answer that and take care of it," Ray said after this had gone on for ten minutes. "I mean, we can't just drive around for the rest of the night. Once we pick up the pizza, we gon' have to go back, and he may still be there," he said, pulling into the parking lot of the pizza place.

"I know, but damn. I didn't want to do this tonight. I didn't want you caught up in my and Devon's drama."

"Don't worry about me. I am a grown-ass man. I know this could get ugly, but believe me, he is not going to step to me like that." He got out to get the pizza.

Leila looked at Deja in the back seat. The baby was sleeping peacefully in her car seat. Her momma's loud conversation hadn't disturbed her.

Leila held her ringing phone and still didn't answer. Maybe Devon would just give up and go home. When they pulled onto her block, he was parked on the street in front of her house. She swallowed hard and took a deep breath as Ray pulled her truck into the driveway. She undid her seat belt and looked over her shoulder. Devon was getting out of his car.

"It's going to be fine," Ray said.

Even though she knew it wasn't the truth, she smiled anyway. She opened her door to get out.

Devon had already reached the truck. "Lei, we need to talk. Now," he demanded, grabbing her arm.

Leila saw Ray move forward slightly, but he didn't say anything. She appreciated him giving her a chance to handle it on her own, and she knew that if things escalated, he would step in. That was the kind of man he was. She turned her attention back to Devon.

"Let me go," she said and snatched away from him.

"Lei," he said through clenched teeth.

"Ray, let me see the keys, please," she said. He handed them to her, and she pointed to a gold key. "This is the house key. You can go on inside," she said, holding the keys back toward him. He didn't move to take them.

Devon moved into her line of sight. "Can we please—"

"Can we please what?" she asked, cutting him off.

He looked toward Ray. "Look," he said, "I just want to get DJ and I'll be on my way."

"Fine. You want your kid? Here ya go," she said, handing Deja to him. "I'm sure you have everything you need at your place for her. Or did you need anything?" she asked, handing him Deja's diaper bag. He had everything from milk to clothes and toys at his place, so she knew he didn't need anything else.

"This is far from being over, believe that," he said and walked away.

He put the baby in her car seat and gave Leila an evil look before he got into his car. She and Ray waited for him to leave before they got the pizza and movies and went inside.

"Oh my God, he's an asshole!" Leila yelled as she locked the door. She wanted to cry. She was so upset and angry that she was shaking by the time she put the movies on the counter and took off her coat.

"Baby, calm down and stop, okay?" Ray said, coming over to her and rubbing her shoulders. "Breathe. Take a deep breath for me and relax."

"Why does he live to torture me, huh?" She started to cry. "What in the fuck does he want from me?" she sobbed.

"Shhh." Ray held her tight while she cried. "Don't cry. It's not so bad, trust me. Come on, deep breath. I can't stand to see you cry."

Leila began to calm down. "I'm sorry," she said. "I didn't want to get you in the middle of my madness."

"It's okay. Nothing happened. Everything is okay," he said.

"I know nothing happened, at least not this time. I don't know why he won't just give me the divorce and move on."

"Because you are beautiful, sexy, and intelligent. And he sees that now. He sees that you are worth loving, and he probably regrets leaving you."

Leila found that hard to believe. He hadn't made her feel worthy of love in so long. She had forgotten how it felt to be wanted, loved, and cared for. Until Ray. In the short time she had been with him, he had given her that feeling again. He cared for her the way she was, and it wasn't based on physical appearance.

"I haven't had any man to love me other than Devon. I know I'm a great person with so much love to give, but I don't know if I'll ever experience someone loving me again."

"That's where you are so wrong. I adore you. Loving you comes easy because you are so wonderful. If you give me a chance to love you, I will love you hard and protect you from pain and all the other bullshit. I'd love to see you carry my babies and care for them like you care for Deja. You don't understand how you have captured my heart in the last couple of months. If you want me, Leila, I'm right here. I love you, and I don't want to be without you."

Leila couldn't move. She knew she and Ray had something good, but she never thought he'd fall for her the way she had fallen for him.

"I love you too, and I do want you. I knew I was in love with you when you kissed Deja and me on the forehead before you went to pack your overnight bag to come over here last night. Hearing that you love me too is like—"

Ray cut her off with a kiss. When he pulled away, he said, "I want you to be happy and not worry about Devon and your past. He will not hurt you again, and I will deal with him being Deja's dad. He isn't going to have you crying and getting upset like this if I can help it. I'm going to be here for you and hold your hand and comfort you when you need it. Don't let him get you down, baby, okay?"

"But you don't know him. Devon is like a rash that keeps on coming back, no matter how much Cortizone you apply."

"And you can keep scratching that rash or let the Cortizone do its job. Let me make it better. I don't want you to continue to let Devon have this type of power over you."

"You're right. I . . . I just don't know how," she stuttered.

"I'm here, okay? It will get easier."

Leila let him hold her for a few moments, and then they grabbed a couple of plates, beer, and the pizza. She put Devon out of her mind and went down to the basement with Ray to watch the movies they had rented. They ate all the bad food they'd bought and enjoyed each other's company. Before they went to bed that night, she declared that they would have a movie night at least once a week.

Chapter Twenty-two

"Devon, why are you dragging this out?" Leila whispered. She was so irritated with Devon she wanted to slap the shit out of him.

They stood with their attorneys in front of the judge.

Devon addressed the judge. "First, Your Honor, I love my wife, and I'm not ready to just call it quits. I feel if given another six months, Leila and I can resolve our differences, and we can get back to loving each other."

"Man, please. That's bullshit and you know it!" Leila yelled. Her attorney put a hand on her arm.

The judge banged his gavel and glared at her. "Motion granted," he said. Leila's mouth dropped open, and her eyes bulged. "I'm giving you six more months, Mr. Vampelt. Until then, this court is adjourned." He banged his gavel again.

"Judge, please, you can't be serious." Leila had tears in her eyes. She couldn't believe he had actually given it another six months.

"Mrs. Vampelt," her attorney said, trying to get her to calm down.

"Walter, you are my lawyer. You have to do something. You know that Devon and I are over. We don't even need another six seconds to figure that out. I am done with him," she cried.

"Mrs. Vampelt, if you continue to behave like you have today, with your outbursts, profanity, and clever comments, disrespecting my court, a six-month reconciliation period will be the least of your worries." The judge stood and left the bench.

Leila hated him. Her attorney tried to talk to her, but she looked away as tears rolled down her cheeks. The smug look on Devon's face made her want to beat the snot out of him.

She sat and cried while everyone left the courtroom. She was so over Devon and their marriage. Just the sight of him made her sick. She'd go to the counseling as the court ordered, but she would sit quietly because she wouldn't change shit at that point. Devon's ridiculous attempts to make it work were a joke. He was now giving her a hard time because he was jealous.

She stood to leave and saw Devon sitting a few rows behind her. *Damn*. She'd thought he left when everyone else did. She tried to walk past him, but he stood and blocked the aisle.

"Lei," he said.

She held up a hand. "Don't. Please don't say shit to me." She turned to go another way, but he didn't let her.

"You know I'm not going to just let you go off and be with this other dude you trying to be with." Arrogance rolled off him in ways as he continued. "You are mine, and you will always be mine."

"You know what, Devon? You can keep telling yourself that lie. This here is over. Done. Finished. I am not yours." She held her hands out to the side. "This belongs to Rayshon Johnson now. He does things to me and my body that you, my dear, were never capable of doing. It's okay that you want to drag this divorce out." She stepped closer to him and kept her voice low. "Just keep in mind that, every night, your wife is being fucked outta her mind by another man."

This time, he didn't stop her from walking away.

When she got home, she was tired as hell. Ray had an early client, so he wasn't coming over, and she had Deja, so she didn't want to go over to his place. She wanted, no, she needed to see him, to be near him. But she couldn't. Renee wasn't available, and she knew there was no way Devon would take of the baby for her after what she'd said to him in the courtroom.

She decided to call it a night, but after she showered and got into bed, she couldn't sleep. She tossed and turned in her bed, thinking of the six-month extension the judge had granted. She was still mad as hell about it. She grabbed her phone and called Ray. She needed to be with him, and she'd just take her little one with her.

"Hey, baby," he said when he picked up.

"Hey, I know it's late, but I gotta come over. I don't wanna be alone tonight," she said.

"Sure, you know you can," he said.

She got up and got her daughter—who was now a year and three months old—grabbed a few items for them both, and headed to his loft. When she knocked on his door, he opened it and helped her with the baby and bags.

"You should have called me from downstairs before you lugged all this up by yourself," he said, putting Deja on the sofa.

"You are so right, because that little girl is heavy," she said, stepping out of her shoes.

Ray sat down and took off Deja's little sweater and gave her a couple of kisses. She laughed and talked to him in her baby talk. Leila left them and went into his room to undress and get comfortable. When she came back, she undressed her baby and put on her pajamas. She put her in her playpen that she had set up, which was where she normally slept when they spent the night over at Ray's place. She had baby items and other items at his place, so she didn't have to carry so much stuff back and forth.

As soon as the baby was asleep, Leila climbed into Ray's bed.

"How did it go?" he asked.

"How did what go?" she asked as if she didn't know what he was talking about. She didn't want to talk about how horribly things had gone.

"You know what I'm talking about," he said, rubbing her arm softly.

"No, I don't," she said, still playing the role.

"Leila, shit, now. You know I'm talking about the hearing with Devon."

"Ray, it was awful, and I'm honestly mortified about it."

"What happened?" he asked, sitting up and turning on the lamp on the nightstand.

She took a deep breath and gave him the play-by-play. When she got to the end, she said, "And the conclusion is he got the six months," she said sadly.

"What? No way." He looked disappointed. "Did you tell that judge that you didn't love him and you have someone else in your life who you love and want to start your life over with?" he asked.

"It doesn't work like that, and the judge hates me. I know he does. No matter what I said or what my attorney argued, he felt it necessary to give Devon another six stupid months, all for nothing. I am not interested in working it out with him."

"This is total bullshit. I can't believe this. This cannot be happening."

"I'm afraid it is," she said, trying not to cry again.

"We have to put our lives on hold for another six months so Devon can walk around feeling good about himself?" he yelled.

"Ray, baby, lower your voice, please. Deja," she said, pointing to the playpen next to the bed.

"I'm sorry. I'm just so upset and angry about this bullshit," he said in a lower voice.

"I know. Trust me, that's exactly how I felt today when the judge said that garbage. But we are not on hold. We are still going to be together and continue to love each other. Devon can't stop that." She rested her head on his lap.

"I know, but I wanted this to be over today so I could give you this." He took a little black velvet box from his nightstand drawer and gave it to her.

"What's this?" she asked, sitting up. She opened the box and found an engagement ring.

"No, no, no. No way, Ray. No," she said, looking at the ring. "You can't be serious. No way can you be serious." She turned and looked at him wide-eyed, unable to say anything else.

"I'm so serious, Leila, and I can't wait another day to ask you. I love you. You are my match, my perfect fit. You and that little girl mean so much to me, and I wanna be with you and have a family. I want to take care of you two."

Leila looked back down at the ring. "I don't know what to say. I never expected something like this"

"Do you love me?" he asked, turning her to face him.

"Yes, I love you. I adore you, and I want to give you all of me. I wanna spend the rest of my days with you, giving you all the love and affection that you've given me. You helped me to get back to me, to see who I am. Only love could make a person do for someone what you have done for me. I've never felt sexier or more wanted or more special by anyone. I am honored that you love me this much." She held up the ring. "I would love to marry you, Mr. Johnson. Yes, yes, yes. My answer is yes."

Ray smiled and pulled her into an embrace before taking the ring box from her. She held out her left hand and let him slide the ring onto her finger.

She hadn't thought anything could make this day better. But Ray did. She may be stuck with Devon's last name for six more months, but she belonged to Ray. She wasn't going to let Devon get under her skin. And in six months, when they saw the judge again, she was going to be as pleasant as possible. The judge would have to grant her divorce.

Chapter Twenty-three

Leila sighed and sat back on the couch. "Devon, what do you want me to say?" she asked.

"I want you to say that you love me and there is a chance for us," he pleaded.

She wanted to laugh. "I can't say that because I don't love you and there is no chance for us." She had told him this more than a dozen times since he had shown up at her house.

Devon threw his hands in the air. "Why? Why can't you just try?"

"We have talked and talked about this. We have gone back and forth with it. I don't want to take this trip down memory lane, and I'm sure you don't want to either. You abandoned me when I was pregnant with your child. You left me too, too many nights crying my eyeballs out. The night I went into labor, you ignored my calls. I was terrified and didn't know what to do. I had to call a friend to come and get me to the hospital. You lied to me in the hospital on the night of your daughter's birth, saying that you would come home and work things out. You never came home, and I got over the fake promises and the lies that you told me. So why, Devon? For the love of God, why can't you let me go and give me the divorce? You didn't want me then, but now you wanna come back?"

"Because I love you, Leila, and I love my child. I have changed. This is no gimmick, no lies, nor fake promises. I love you, and I want our marriage. I want one final chance to show you that I'm ready to make it right. I want us to work, so please reconsider and give us a chance to start over."

"Why now?" she snapped. "Because I'm not so disgusting to look at anymore? Or because you know someone else loves me?"

"He doesn't love you."

"What? You don't know anything about him. You don't know shit about us, and you don't have a clue what loving me is about. You wanted little Barbie doll Michelle and couldn't love me for who I am, so you just assume Ray doesn't love me either." It was her turn to plead. "Why don't you just give me the divorce so we both can move on?"

"Because Michelle will never measure up to you," he answered.

"What, she can't seem to pour her heart into you and put her own needs to the side while giving you all you need? She can't give you two hundred percent of what you need like I did for years while you gave me the finger?"

"You were the best woman I've ever had. Everything about you was good. You were so loving, sensitive, and kind. You loved me with everything in you." He shook his head. "And I want that again. I need that again,"

Leila thought back to how she used to do everything for him. She took care of him like a wife was supposed to, but he stopped taking care of her.

"Look," she said, "I know how you feel because I have been in your shoes. When I begged and begged you to work things out, for you to come home and give our marriage a chance, you wouldn't do that for me. You drove me away. You pushed and lied and made empty promises. And I don't wanna be married to you anymore. Please, please, please, why won't you give me a divorce?"

"Because I can't. I just can't. I don't want to let you go. I can't let you go. I was wrong. I was a horrible husband, and I want to make it up to you. I want our marriage back. I want you back," he cried. "You are my wife, and I want to come back home."

She looked up at the ceiling to keep from crying, then looked back at him. "You don't have me anymore."

He put his head down and didn't speak for a moment. Finally he said, "I understand that I hurt you. I made a huge mistake, but I love you so much, baby." He looked at her with watery eyes. "And you can't tell me that you don't love me anymore. I won't accept that."

"Devon, please," she said. She didn't want to be cold. As much as he had hurt her, she didn't like seeing him in so much pain.

"You want me to beg? I'm begging you. Please, can you give us another try?"

She felt for him, but her mind was made up. She was engaged to another man, and there was absolutely no chance for her and Devon.

"I'm sorry. There is nothing else to discuss." She stood and went upstairs, leaving him crying on the sofa.

In her bedroom, she sat on her ottoman and cried for both of them. She hated waiting for Devon to do what she knew he knew was the right thing to do. It wasn't going to happen that day. At that point, she wasn't sure if he was going to give in at all.

She prayed and asked God to help them. She prayed for Devon to accept her decision and sign the papers to give her the divorce. She wanted to marry Ray and start their life together.

Chapter Twenty-four

"Hold on," Ray said, rushing to the door. It was two in the morning, and he wondered who could be knocking on his door at that time of night. He turned on the lamp on the end table and looked through the peephole.

"You gotta be kidding me," he said when he saw Katrina on the other side of the door. He hesitated and took a deep breath before he opened the door.

"Hey," she said softly.

"What do you mean, hey? And what are you doing here at this hour, Kat?" he asked. He wasn't sure he wanted to hear her answer.

"I wanted to say thanks for helping me and to tell you I found a spot and that you helped save my job." She shifted her stance. "Can I come in?" she asked.

He sighed, wanting to say no. But he was a gentleman. "Sure, but you can't stay long."

She came in and sat on the sofa. Ray sat in the chair and watched her. He saw her looking at his pictures of Leila and Deja on the coffee table.

"Who's the beautiful little girl?" she asked as if Leila were not in the picture too.

"That is Deja, my fiancée's daughter."

"Fiancee?" she spat and tilted her head.

"Yes," Ray confirmed.

She clicked her tongue. "Her baby is gorgeous," she said.

"Yeah, she looks so much like her beautiful mom," he said. "Why are you here, Kat?"

"Like I said, I wanted to say thanks," she said, still looking around. "Wow, this new lady in your life must be special. I don't remember you ever displaying this many pictures of me or us when we were together."

"She is. And you're welcome. Now, why are you really here?"

Katrina stood. "Don't be so suspicious. I wanted to give you a proper thank-you, and I wanted to do it in person." She moved over to a wall unit, examining Leila's picture. She unzipped her jacket and took it off, revealing a sexy low-cut top. She sat back down and gave him an inviting stare.

"What are you doing?" he asked. "I'm engaged and I'm happy."

She picked up the picture from the coffee table. "This is the woman you're planning to marry?"

"Yes, that's Leila."

"You've changed," she said, putting the picture back.

He frowned. "Changed how?"

"You know, your taste in women. I never pictured you with a big girl."

"You don't know me like you thought you did. And my woman is a full-figured queen. Big girl, thick sista, plus-size, or whatever you want to call it, she is my superstar, and I share a life with her that I know I wouldn't have had with you." *Who is she to talk about anyone when her shit isn't all that?*

"You know, you're right. I fucked up, and I made a lot of horrible choices that caused me a hell of a lot of grief. But you know what? I'm finally at the point in my life where I can own up to my bullshit. Hurting you was one of my biggest mistakes, and I'm sorry," she said, sitting on the edge of the sofa. "I know I can't change my past, but I have control of my future, and it wouldn't be worth living without you in it."

Ray wanted to laugh in her face. He didn't have a future or anything else with Katrina, and he preferred to never see her again. "You got to be kidding me," he said, shaking his head.

"I'm not kidding, Ray. I'm here to ask you to give me another chance."

"You may wanna change your brand of crack or get you a new dealer," he said, fighting the urge to laugh.

"I'm not on drugs, and I am dead serious. You were the best thing that ever happened to me. I've never stopped loving you. I think about you and us all the time, and I would like to start over and be the woman I should have been back then for you. I'm older and wiser and smarter, and I am ready to love you the way you deserve to be loved."

"Okay, Kat, if you aren't high or taking any kind of drugs, you must be plain old crazy. I just told you that I am engaged. I am in love with this woman," he said, pointing to the picture on the coffee table. "So how does your brain tell you to open your mouth and talk about us getting back together?"

"My heart is what tells me to speak. If I don't open my mouth and express how much I love you and how much I want us to be together, how would you know?"

"Well, now that I know, the answer is no. I don't know who you think you are or what you take me for, but you can't just walk back into my life and tell me you want to act right and e pect me to just drop everything and say, 'Okay, let's pick up where we left off.' It doesn't work like that. Now you wanna come back after all the pain you put me through? After I'm happy with someone else? No, Kat. No."

"Why not? Because of her?" she said, pointing to Leila's picture.

"Yes, because of her. What are you talking about?" he asked. *This chick has to be crazy.* He spoke slowly to make sure she understood. "She and I are engaged."

"You will never love another woman like you loved me. No way do you have with her the passion, the emotions, or the happiness you had with me. You don't, do you?"

"You know, I don't," he said. She smiled at his answer, but the smile dropped at his next words. "I have more love, more passion, and more happiness with her than I had with you. Leila has this power over me, sorta like a love spell, that I never had with you." Now he smiled. "And you know what else? Leila is honest, so I can rest easy at night knowing that our love is strong, that she is not off somewhere sharing my goods with some other cat. Something I couldn't say about you."

Tears filled Katrina's eyes. "You're right. I was an unfaithful, lying bitch, and trust me, I've paid for my mistakes. I know that I messed our thing up, and I'm sorry." She drew her feet up and began to sob.

Ray let her cry. After a while, she fell asleep. He didn't want her to stay, but it was late, so he got her a blanket. Then he went to his room and got in bed, wondering why he was allowing her to sleep on his sofa again.

Chapter Twenty-five

The next morning, Christa showed up ten minutes late. Ray had been hoping she wouldn't show at all. Katrina was still asleep on the sofa when she arrived.

When they got upstairs and had started her workout, she asked, "What's up with your guest on the couch?"

"Why are you always minding my business?" he asked.

"You know I'm the kind of person who says what's on my mind. That chick on the couch doesn't look anything like Leila. I'm nosy, so I asked."

"Well, Miss Honest, she is an old friend," he said, leaving it at that.

"Hmm. She's a pretty old friend. Does your woman know this pretty old friend is on your couch?" she asked as she finished her last sit-up.

"Christa, please. Why can't you come and enjoy your workout without asking a million questions or talking about folks' business?"

She paused before she spoke. "I don't know. I'm sorry." She put her head down.

She had absolutely nothing important in her life to be excited about, so she lived to be in other folks' business, Ray figured.

"Look, I gotta get ready for my next client," he said, grabbing the sweaty towel from the floor and tossing it in the hamper. He continued to wipe the equipment down, and Christa walked down the steps without saying bye.

When Katrina heard the front door shut, she got up and went to the bathroom. She smiled at her reflection in the mirror. She had managed to lay her head in Ray's loft that night and didn't have to sleep in her car. She had three more nights to find a place to rest her head until her apartment was ready.

She had finally managed to get back on her feet, but all her cash had been used to pay deposits and utilities. She had a few dollars left for gas and to get groceries when she got into her apartment. She didn't have enough for that and a hotel room. She had to bide her time for a couple more days, and she hoped to do that here. She hated all the pictures of Leila and wished he was still single, not engaged. His things were still in the places they were before, and it felt like old times. After she freshened up, she went into the kitchen. She heard Ray upstairs with his next client.

She opened the fridge and grabbed the juice and toasted a bagel. She looked at the clock. Ray would be another forty-five minutes, so she ran down and got her bag from her car. She went into Ray's master bedroom to shower instead of going to the hall shower. She wanted space to be able to shave her legs and enjoy her shower. When she finished, she got out, wrapped a towel around her body, and went into his room to put lotion on. The music was still going upstairs, meaning he was still working, so she took her time. She wanted him to get a look at her body in the towel, so she didn't bother getting dressed.

A little while later, she heard the front door open and close. *Ray must have finished his session.* She looked up when he stepped into the bedroom.

"What are you doing?" he asked her.

"Putting on lotion," she said.

"I can see the obvious, Kat. What are you doing in my room? You know there is a shower in the other bathroom."

"I know, but this one is so much bigger," she said, moving around like she was in her own house.

"You can't just come into my room and used my shower." He opened his mouth to say something else but stopped when he heard a knock on the door. He looked at his watch. "Look, just hurry," he said and left the room.

She heard him and his client go upstairs. She didn't change her pace. She was in no hurry to get dressed. She began to snoop around the room and smiled to see that Ray still used condoms. At least he wasn't trying to make babies with Leila, she thought.

She was stepping into her thong when she heard a knock on the door. She wrapped the towel back around her and went to answer it. She went up on her tiptoes and looked through the peephole. Her eyes lit up when she saw Leila. She tossed her hair and opened the door.

"Baby, I forgot my key," were the first words from Leila's mouth, but she stopped talking when she saw her.

Katrina was pleased when Leila's smile dropped, and her mouth hung open. "Can I help you?" she asked, blocking the door.

"Hi, I'm Leila. Is Ray in?"

"Yes, but he's busy," she said, adjusting her towel and still not moving.

"Well, I'm his fiancée, so would you mind?" she asked, trying to move forward.

Katrina didn't budge. "I know this may be a little awkward, and I probably shouldn't be the one to tell you, but I'm Katrina. I'm not sure if Ray ever mentioned me, but we were engaged once. We recently started talking again, and well, you know how things are. We're working on getting back together. I'm sure Ray will call you soon," she said. She hid a smile at the panicked look on Leila's face and watched as she turned and walked away without saying anything.

Chapter Twenty-six

Leila turned and headed for the elevator. When she got to her truck, she sat in it and cried. She called Ray's cell, and of course, it went straight to his voicemail. She had known he would be in a session when she went, but she had to get a bag with price tags and a few other items for the store from his place before she opened that morning.

How could Ray hook up with Katrina just like that without any warning or mention that he was even thinking about it? There hadn't been a single sign that he was even considering hooking up with his ex. Why hadn't he told her instead of cheating on her? He had told her all about her, so she knew the woman wasn't lying about being his ex-fiancee. She was gorgeous. *She probably seduced him with her flawless body.* Her plus-size frame was the last thing he would have thought about with Katrina in front of him.

She started her truck and drove to her store, trying to get her thoughts together. Katrina had caught her off guard, and she wished she had handled the situation differently. She should have pushed her way in and run up the steps and confronted him instead of allowing Katrina to keep her out in the hall.

The store opened, and customers started arriving. She felt like she was moving in slow motion and was happy to see her employee Nicki walk through the door. She had to get inside of her office before the tears she had been fighting all morning came out.

"Hey, Nicki," she said. "I'm so glad you're here. I've got a ton of papers on my desk that I need to go through."

Nicki put her purse and keys down under the counter. "Okay, I'll be fine. I'll let you know if we get busy."

Leila barely made it to her office before the tears started. She sat behind her desk and tried to call Ray again, but she got the voicemail again. When she put the phone down, it rang, and she grabbed it. It was Devon. She took a deep breath. She didn't want to talk to him, but he had Deja, so she had to take his call.

"Hello," she answered.

"Hey, what's going on?"

"Work. I'm at the store. What do you need?"

"Nothing, I was just calling to see what you were doing for lunch. DJ wanted to treat you," he said.

"When did DJ get a job or earn money to be able to treat me to lunch?" she asked smartly.

"Well, Deja gets by on her good looks," he joked.

She got angry. "Listen, my daughter is not going to be some hottie who gets by just on her looks. Don't even think of planting that garbage in my daughter's head," she snapped.

"Hold on, Lei, I was only joking. What's wrong with you?"

"I'm sorry. I'm just tired and frustrated," she said. She swiveled in her chair.

"It's more than that," he said. "I know you. What's bothering you?"

"Nothing. I just can't do lunch with you guys today, okay?" she said, holding back tears.

"Why not?"

"I have a lot going on today, and I'm not going to be able to break free for lunch." She wished he'd stop pushing.

"Okay, we'll see you later, then," he said.

Leila was glad to get off the phone. She tried Ray again and got his voicemail again. She dialed his house phone and froze when Katrina answered. She was so shocked to hear her voice that she just hung up. She didn't even answer his phone, and they were supposed to be engaged.

She felt ill. She had to go home. She wasn't fit to be at the store. She wouldn't get anything done. She grabbed her purse and keys and went out front.

"Nicki, I have to go, okay?" she said. "My head is banging in the worst way. I have to go home. Do you think you can handle the store alone 'til Renee comes in?" She had never left Nicki alone, but she had no choice.

"Sure, it's kinda slow anyway. You go on home. I can manage."

"Call me if you have any questions, okay?"

"I will," Nicki said. "Feel better."

"Thanks."

Leila left the store and got into her truck. As soon as she started the engine, she began to cry again. She managed to make it home without crashing and went straight to her wine cooler. She poured herself a glass and turned on some music. She sang along to Rihanna's "Take a Bow" and then called Ray again. She tried to catch him at the top of the hour before he got started on his next client, but she got voicemail on his cell phone and then the answering machine on his home phone. She threw her phone and went and got the wine bottle. She cried her way through two more glasses and dozed off.

The ringing of her cell phone woke her up, and she got up to get it from the love seat where it landed when she tossed it. She looked at the caller ID, and her heart raced.

It was Ray.

Chapter Twenty-seven

"You have to go," Ray told Katrina after he let his last client out.

"Excuse me?" she asked, frowning.

"'Excuse me'? What's 'excuse me?' You've been here all damn day. I've been so busy, but I told you hours ago to bounce. You gotta roll."

She took a sip of her drink. "Why? Are you expecting someone and don't want me to be here?"

"No, you just have to leave. We are not tight, close, or cool, so you have to go."

"So, you're putting me out?"

"If that's what you want to call it. You have chilled here all day. You showered, ate, lounged around, and now you're drinking mixed drinks. You're not about to be too drunk to drive, so finish your little drink and go." He was not going to let her spend another night. "I have a woman, and she would not like you hanging out over here like we're roomies."

"Oh yeah. She came by this morning," Katrina said casually. She took another sip of her drink.

"Who came by where?" Ray asked, his brow arched and head tilted.

"Leila. Her," she said, pointing to Leila's photo.

"When?" he yelled. He moved close to her. He had never hit a woman, but it looked like Katrina was going to be the first one he ever slapped.

"About seven thirtyish this morning." She took another sip of her cocktail and looked at him.

Seven-thirty this morning? That was during Angela's session, around the time he'd had words with Kat for using his shower after Patricia left.

His jaw tightened. "Tell me you didn't go to my fucking door in a motherfucking bath towel." *Please,* he prayed silently.

"Well, Ray, I heard the door, and I answered it. I didn't know it would be her."

"In a towel? In a towel, Katrina? Why didn't you come and get me? Why didn't you let her in?" he yelled. He stood over her, restraining himself from yanking her ass.

"You were upstairs with your client, and when she saw me, she just left. She didn't ask to come in. I only recognized her from her pictures," she said and took another sip.

"Oh shit. What in the hell is wrong with you?" he yelled.

"What? And why are you yelling? I didn't do anything."

He wanted to knock the innocent look right off her face, but he knew he couldn't. His momma didn't raise him like that. Instead, he said, "You know what? Get up." He took the drink out of her hand and grabbed her arm. "Get your things and get the hell out of my house," he ordered, giving her a slight push.

She stood looking at him.

He set the glass on the table. "I'm not fucking around. Get yo' shit and get the hell out!" he yelled. He went around the living room, collecting her personal items she had left lying around.

"Ray, come on now. Don't just throw me out. I didn't do anything. And I need to stay just one more night. Please."

"You leaving is not optional. You are crazy, and if you did anything to mess things up with my lady and me, I promise you . . ." he said, getting in her face.

"Fine, fine. I'll leave. Just let me get the rest of my things."

He sat on the sofa and put his hands on the top of his head. How had he managed to allow Katrina to screw with him again? He was so done with her. He vowed that if she ever came knocking at his door again, he would never let her in again.

After what seemed like an eternity, she finally came out with her bag. "I'm gone," she said, standing near the door.

"Bye," he said and didn't look up. As soon as she was on the other side of the door, he called Leila.

"What?" she said when she picked up the phone.

"Leila, baby, please tell me that you don't believe whatever Katrina told you this morning," he said.

"Tell me how I'm supposed to think anything other than what that tramp said? She came to the door in a fucking towel, Rayshon, with wet hair. She had a smirk on her face, and she was guarding the entryway like she was the mistress of the house. And you come calling me damn near eleven hours later," Leila spat.

"I promise you that nothing happened between Katrina and me. Whatever she told you, I promise, were lies. I'm just now calling you because I didn't know you came here, and I had back-to-back appointments all day. I would have called you at lunch, but I didn't get one today because Royce, one of my Thursday clients, needed to get in because he's going out of town or some shit. Nothing happened," he said.

"Whatever. Why was the trick there in the first place if nothing is going on? Why was she in a damn towel? Why wouldn't she let me in, even after I told her who I was? Why would she lie and say that you guys were working on getting back together? Why would she do that?"

"She said that? That is not what happened."

"Why was she there?"

He heard her start crying. "A few months back, when I told you I had a friend in trouble, it was Katrina. She had lost her mom and had some issues and didn't have a place to go. I helped her out, and she came by last night just to say thanks."

"Last night? You let her spend the fucking night? That tramp slept over last night?"

"It wasn't like you think. She slept on the sofa. I didn't touch that woman. When you came, I was upstairs with Angela. I guess that's when she used the shower. I didn't know she was showering, for one, and she didn't tell me you came by until about twenty minutes ago."

"So, not only did she spend the night, but she's been chilling at your house all day? That's why she answered the phone when I called."

"She answered my phone?" he asked, shocked.

"Yeah, she did." Leila's voice had gone cold. "Now that I have heard your story, leave me alone." She hung up.

***

Leila sat sobbing. Her phone rang, and she picked it up to hit the button to ignore the call again. Ray had been calling back-to-back since she'd hung up on him. She looked at the caller ID. This time it was Devon.

"Hello," she answered. She heard her voice crack.

"Lei, what's wrong?" he asked.

"I'm sick, okay? I really don't feel well. Can you manage DJ one more night, please?"

"What is it, baby? You sound horrible."

"I know. Can you please, please keep Deja?" she cried.

"Yeah, sure, sure. Are you going to be all right? Are you sure you don't want me to come over?"

"No, I'm not sure. I do need you," she cried. "I need you to come home."

"I'm on my way," Devon said.

It didn't take him long to get there. He led her to the couch and sat holding her. She told him she had a headache and didn't feel well. He didn't say anything for a while, then asked, "What did he do to you, sweetheart?"

Leila didn't answer. She just closed her eyes and cried in his arms.

Chapter Twenty-eight

Ray couldn't fall asleep. He was upset about what went down with him and Leila and was pissed at himself for letting Katrina in. He knew if he saw her again, he'd kill her ass for sure. How had she managed to hurt him again? She was breaking his heart by sabotaging his relationship with the woman he loved. He had prayed and called Leila for thirty minutes straight with no answer. If he lost her over that bullshit, he'd go insane. He lay on the sofa and flipped through TV channels, looking for something to watch.

The next morning, a knock at the door woke him up. He was still on the sofa. He realized he hadn't heard his alarm from the bedroom and had overslept. He got up, went to the door, and opened it for Sonja, his first appointment for the day. He told her to go up and get started on the treadmill, and he'd be with her shortly. He hurried and brushed his teeth and washed his face, then threw on his workout gear and ran upstairs.

Before he knew it, it was time for Leila's session. They didn't work out the traditional way. They worked out in other ways. He spent the hour making her feel good. Since her appointment was at eleven and his lunch was at noon, they had two hours to take a bath together, massage each other, or just sit around. He figured she wouldn't show up.

He was in the kitchen when he heard the knock at the door. When he opened it, he was pleasantly surprised to see her. "Come on in," he said, moving aside.

"I'm not staying. I just came to get my things for the store," she said, walking past him. "I'll get the rest of my stuff later."

"Please wait," he said, following her. She kept moving. "Stop, Lei," he yelled.

She stopped and looked down at the floor. "I just need my things for my store."

"Nothing happened."

She looked up at him with tear-filled eyes. "Save it, okay? Just save it," she said.

He grabbed her arms. "Please listen to me. I would never do that to you. I love you, Leila. Nothing happened. I would never do anything to hurt you."

"No, I thought you would never do anything to hurt me, but you did. I know what I saw." The tears she'd been holding in fell, and seeing them ate him up.

"She slept on the fucking sofa. I made a mistake, baby, but the only mistake was trying to be nice to that bitch and letting her into my home. I swear that I didn't touch that woman." He rubbed his hands up and down her arms. "You know me, baby. You know me. There are women in and out of here every day, so why would I go back to Katrina? Please think. She is an evil, lying—" He stopped himself. He didn't want to think about Katrina. He just wanted to get through to Leila.

"Look at me," he said, lifting her head. "I only want you. I love you, and no woman can come up in here and replace you. I would never lie to you. She was here, and yes, she spent the night, but not with me. I love you, Leila. I only want you," he said and kissed her on the forehead.

"I want to believe you, I do. But why would she stand there and make that shit up?"

"Leila, that woman is twisted. She sat here and examined your picture, and I told her how you were so much better for me and how much better my relationship is with you than what I had with her. She knew about you. I guess she was just jealous. I don't know. What I do know is that I love you more than anything." He pulled her to him and kissed her, using his mouth to emphasize his words.

They ended up in his bed. Ray pulled her clothes off, desperate to please her, to show her how much he loved her. When he slid inside her warmth, it felt like home. Their love-making was frantic and satisfying. Before he knew it, their time was up.

He kissed Leila one more time and left her to relax while he got up to shower and get ready for his next client.

She rolled over and grabbed a pillow. Something red caught her eye. She reached over and pulled it. It was a lace thong. She dropped it and sat up. Another flash of color caught her eye. There was smeared lipstick on the pillow she was holding. She leaped out of bed.

"Ray, you are a fucking liar!" she yelled. She heard the shower turn off.

"What?" he yelled from the bathroom.

"You are a fucking liar," she yelled again. She started crying. "I hate you. You stood in my face and lied to me."

Ray came out of the bathroom, naked and dripping wet. "What's wrong? What are you talking about?"

"This." She threw the thong at him. It hit him in the chest and fell to the floor.

"What is this?" he asked as he bent over and picked it up. "Where did this come from? I've never seen this a day in my life, honey."

She shook her head. "I can't fucking believe you!" She looked around for her clothes and saw something shiny on the floor by the nightstand. She picked it up. It was an earring.

"Lei, please," Ray said. "Where did you get this? Kat must have dropped it. I don't know."

"Oh yeah? She dropped it between your headboard and the mattress? Did she drop this too?" she asked, throwing the earring on the bed. "Oh yeah, and is this the pillow she had her face in when you were hitting it from the back?"

"Katrina must have done all of this garbage yesterday. I didn't even sleep here last night. I slept on the sofa. Do you think I'd get up and fix my bed and not notice a pair of underwear, a soiled pillowcase, and an earring?"

Leila didn't want to hear it. She dressed quickly, stuffed her panties and bra in her purse, and went into the living room. Ray followed her, still naked.

"Leila," he said as she grabbed her bags of things for the store. "Lei, baby," he said. She kept moving. "Leila," he said, blocking her path.

"Move. I will come by this weekend for the rest of my things. It's over. You are a liar." She

went around him and snatched the door open.
Mia, his one o'clock appointment, stood with her
hand raised to knock.

"Hi, Mia," Leila said. "He's all yours."

She walked away, leaving Mia staring open-
mouthed at Ray in all his naked glory.

Chapter Twenty-nine

Leila got into her truck, heated and heartbroken. She drove in circles, then headed toward home, confused and hurt. Rayshon Johnson was a two-timing, lying-ass dog who had played her. She had let him play her. He could have been lying to her from the very beginning, she thought as she pulled into her driveway.

She was a mess, and the scent of their lovemaking on her body pissed her off more. She undressed and got into the shower to wash Ray off her. She cursed him, yelled, and cried as she scrubbed herself. By the time she was done with her shower, she had an excruciating headache. She had to talk to someone, so she called Renee after she alerted Devon that she was home early. Renee was with a customer, so she couldn't talk.

Leila busied herself doing little things around the house, and before long, she heard a car pull into her driveway. It was Devon bringing Deja home. She ran to the bathroom and washed her face, but she couldn't hide her swollen, red eyes.

She let them in, picked up her baby, and held her tight. She kissed her ten times before putting her down.

"I brought your favorite Chinese food," Devon said. "Are you feeling better today?" he asked as he followed her into the kitchen

"I'm fine," she said, not wanting to talk to him. She hated him being so nice to her and acting so concerned.

"You don't look fine," he said, washing his hands at the sink. "Sit down, and I'll fix you and DJ a plate."

"I can do it," she said.

"Lei, sit down, okay?" he said.

Leila didn't argue. She put Deja in her high chair and sat down. Devon put a plate in front of her. She picked over her food and tried not to cry in front of him.

"Look, I'm not too hungry. I'm going upstairs," she said.

She went to her room, got into bed, and just let the tears drop. About an hour later, Devon came up.

"Are you sleeping?" he asked.

"No," she said.

"What did he do to you?" Devon asked again.

"I don't want to talk right now."

To her surprise, he didn't push. He pulled the door closed and left her alone. A few moments later, Renee called her back.

"Hey, girl, what's going on?" she asked.

"Oh, Renee, my life is so fucked up," Leila cried.

"What happened? What's wrong?"

"Everything," Leila said. "Ray cheated on me with his ex."

"No," Renee said. "No way."

"Yes, ma'am. I caught her over there yesterday. This morning, I went by there, and I let him convince me that what I saw yesterday wasn't true. After we made love, I found that ho's panties in the sheets."

"Damn, what did he say?"

"Said some shit about her putting them there on purpose like I'm a damn fool."

"Well, that is something to consider. I mean, Ray is a good guy."

"Come on. If your husband told you that, would you believe him?"

"I guess not. It's just hard to believe. I mean, Ray is romantic, kind, and he is so good to you. For him to just up and cheat . . . I don't know."

"That's why I don't think it's his first time. Hell, who knows how many of them hoes he's been with?"

"I don't believe that. As big as them tricks' mouths are, one of them would have been put him on Front Street."

Leila thought about it. It made sense. Rayshon had never hesitated to make it known to any of his female clients that he was with her. "Yeah, maybe so," she said. "But I don't know what to do now."

"Just please tell me you're not considering going back to Devon."

"Are you crazy? I'm hurt, but I'm not stupid."

"I'm just saying. When you are emotional and going through it, that's when you are weak when it comes to Devon."

"Devon and I are history," Leila said. "We are done, and I wouldn't take him back if a million Rays cheated on me," she said with a little laugh.

Devon had done her in and made too many fake-ass promises. Going back to him would be going back to hell. He had lied and let her down too many times, and she wasn't going to allow him another opportunity to hurt her, no matter how much he thought he had changed. Devon was not an option.

When they got off the phone, Leila pulled the covers up to her chin and lay in the darkness Ray called and called, and she finally powered off her cell phone and unplugged her house phone. Every time she had been tempted to answer, the image of Katrina in a towel entered her mind. She felt like a fool for giving in to him earlier.

She got up, turned the light on, and looked at herself in the mirror. Why had he felt it necessary to mess around with his ex? Was it the way she looked? Because she wasn't as sexy and beautiful as Katrina was? She was a Freddie Jackson, while Katrina was a Janet Jackson. She felt tears begin to form again. She hated her body, and Ray hadn't made her feel any better by cheating on her with Miss America. *Maybe he'd want me if I didn't have these rolls here or if my thighs were slimmer or my breasts were perky,* she thought as she pulled, stretched, and poked her skin.

"That's why you want her over me," she said out loud. "Just like Devon wanted Michelle over me."

She wiped her tears and moved away from the mirror. She took a deep breath and went down to see her baby. She was disappointed when Devon told her that Deja was already sleeping.

"You don't have to hang around, Devon. I'm good," she said.

"I know your man did something to hurt you. You can talk to me. I don't like seeing you like this."

"Oh, really? I guess it was fine when you had me like this. You don't remember me being like this over you? You can't recall when you had me like this day in and out? But Ray has me like this, and you hate it?"

"You know what I mean. I fucked up, yes. And I didn't like seeing you like this then either. You don't deserve to be sad and hurt or upset by me or any other man, okay? I'm not happy about what I did to you or the bullshit I put you through."

"Devon, please. Worry about your own issues and don't concern yourself with my issues with Ray. You did a number on me too, remember? I am a lot stronger now, thanks to you, and I'm going to bounce back. So please spare me." She went into the kitchen to get a drink, and he followed her.

"I know I did a number on you and our relationship. I'm paying for it every day. Every night that I can't come home to you or have you the way I want to have you, I'm paying for it. I know I can't dog your man out for whatever it is he has done, but I do care about you and your happiness. Don't think for one moment that I wouldn't be concerned or worried about you. I told you months ago that I never want to see you cry or hurt again. Seeing you like this and not being able to make you feel better is killing me."

"Excuse me," she said and ran upstairs. She took her glass of wine with her. She couldn't stand him trying to be so good when he used to be so bad. She sat on the ottoman and sipped her wine. She felt like screaming. Why was her life such a rollercoaster, filled with so many emotions? Devon was cruel, and Ray had come along and removed the dark clouds. Now Ray was the storm, and Devon was trying to be her sunshine.

She polished off the rest of her drink and climbed into bed. A couple of hours later, Devon came to her bedroom door. She wished he would just go home and leave her alone.

"Lei," he whispered.

"Yeah?" she replied.

"Can I come in?" he asked.

She rolled her eyes. "Sure." She knew he wasn't going to leave her alone.

He climbed in bed with her, and she kept her back to him. Her sniffing was the only sound in the room.

"What did he do to you, sweetheart?" Devon asked again.

"Why doesn't anyone want me?" she asked.

"That's crazy."

"No, it's not crazy. Am I just that hideous and disgusting that I can't keep a man interested?

As soon as the perfect size five appears, I'm forgotten."

"That's not true. That's nonsense. I want you."

She rolled over to face him. "You want me now, but when you had me, you didn't want me."

"I was a fool. I messed up, but trust me, my love, you are incredibly beautiful. When I first laid eyes on you, I couldn't get you outta my mind. I couldn't think of another woman. I had to have you. Don't you remember when we were in college how I followed you everywhere and begged you to go out with me? I asked about a million times, and when you finally said yes, I think I did the Running Man all the way back to my dorm. You are so smart and brave and strong and good. If I had been the man I was supposed to be and cherished you, I would be looking at your beautiful face every morning.

"I was so busy focusing on images and too busy looking at the type of women the other executives had on their arms 'til I forgot about how beautiful the woman I already had was. I got lost in that bullshit, Lei. I'm so sorry for what I put you through and what you are going through now. Whomever this cat is choosing to be with over you, it has nothing to do with the way you look, okay? So get that out of your mind. You are beautiful, Leila, you are. I know I may have messed up your head with the insults and all the garbage I said to you about your weight, but I was wrong."

"I know you're sorry. I just don't know why every time I fall in love, I end up losing my man to another woman."

"You're not losing. We're the ones who lost. If your relationship ended with this Ray guy over him and another woman, it has nothing to do with your looks. I'll bet you any amount of money he is going to realize that choosing another over you was the biggest mistake of his life."

Leila closed her eyes and let Devon hold her. It felt nice to be in his arms, even if it was just as friends.

Chapter Thirty

Ray was going out of his mind. He'd strangle Katrina if he saw her again. How in the world was he going to get Leila back after she found panties, an earring, and makeup on his pillow? Katrina really fucked him for sure, he thought as he paced the floor. The towel scene was the work of an evil bitch. He couldn't believe that after all he had done to help her, she'd obliterate his relationship. He tried not to cry, but he broke down after his hundredth attempt to call Leila.

For the first time since he started his own business, he was on the phone canceling appointments. He knew he'd be no good the next day. He couldn't function because of his fear that she was out of his life for good. He called her, texted her, and emailed her, but she didn't reply. He paced, cried, yelled, and threw things across the room. He went a few rounds with his punching bag and ran four miles on the tread-mill, but he was still too wound up to shut his

eyes. He called Leila again, and when she still
didn't answer, he grabbed his keys and drove to
her house.

His heart dropped into the pit of his stomach
when he saw Devon's car in her driveway. "Son
of a bitch!" he yelled angrily. Tears burned his
eyes. Why would she run back to him? Why
would she tell him that she didn't want Devon,
but as soon as they broke up, she was right back
with him? He contemplated ringing the doorbell,
but he knew that that would make things even
worse. He sat watching the house for hours.
All the lights were out, as though a family had
retired for the night. Devon was there for the
night.

Ray hated everyone: himself for allowing
Katrina to come in, Katrina for being such an
evil bitch, Leila for running back to Devon, and
Devon for being there for her. He clenched the
steering wheel and forced himself to crank
the engine and drive back to his loft. He asked
God to put Katrina on the road so he could run
her ass over, but he knew that wasn't going to
happen. He cried and drove home, feeling like
he had just been in a plane crash.

By the time he turned the key to his loft, he
was in horrible shape. He was glad that his
clients understood that he had to cancel. There
was no way he would make it through the day.

The next morning, there was a knock on Ray's door. He jumped and looked at the clock. It was five in the morning. He went to the door, hoping it was Leila but knowing it wasn't. It was Christa.

"Hey," she said.

"Christa?" he said, surprised to see her.

"Aren't you going to let me in?"

"You didn't get my message?" he asked.

"What message?"

"About me canceling our appointment today. I talked to your roommate. When I called, she said you were in the shower."

"Oh, well, by the time I got out, she was gone, so I didn't get the message," she said.

"Come on in, I guess." He held the door open for her. "I'm sorry, but I am going to need a minute."

"That's fine. I don't have much to do this morning." She came in and sat on the sofa. "Your place is a mess," she said as he left the room. When he came back twenty minutes later, she said, "Are you okay? What's wrong? I've never seen you this unprofessional before, and your place is crazy, man."

"This isn't a good time." He sat down on the chair.

"What happened? What's going on? Did someone die?" she asked.

Ray hesitated. Normally, he would never talk to Christa about his personal life, but he needed to talk to somebody.

"We broke up." He blinked back tears. "Leila and I broke up."

"What? Why? What happened?"

"The pretty girl on the couch is what happened."

"What did she do?"

"Let's just say she fucked me," he said, letting the tears fall.

"I'm sorry. I can't imagine what she could have done to break up your relationship with Leila. I mean, she slept on your sofa. That's not grounds for a breakup, in my opinion."

"She did a little more than that." He wiped his face.

"What? You didn't mess with her, did you?"

"Hell no. I love Leila. You of all people know that."

"I do, but it doesn't make sense to me."

"This is what went down." He told her the entire story. By the end, she was sitting with her hand over her mouth.

She shook her head. "I've got to admit, I've done some trifling things in my life too, but that bitch is certifiably bogus. My God, Ray, I'm sorry. That is fucked up."

"Yep. But I guess I got what I deserved." He put his head down.

"No, that is not true. You are a good man. I know that you love Leila, and I don't believe for one second that you would do that to her. I'm so sorry, man."

"Thanks," he said and got up.

He put on a pot of coffee, and he and Christa talked for several hours. He felt a little better after talking to her but was worried about her tendency to gossip.

"Now, Christa," he said, "I know you know a lot of my clients, but please don't go telling my business. I talked to you this morning, not you and your girlfriends."

"I respect you, and I promise I will not share our conversation with anyone." She got up, and he walked her to the door.

"Thanks for listening," he said.

"Anytime. And again, I am sorry about you and Leila. She's a good woman, and you two deserve each other."

Ray smiled. "I just hope I can get her back."

"All things happen for a reason. And she loves you. If you guys are meant to be, no matter how much time goes by, you will be together." He nodded, and she patted him on the arm. "If you need anything, let me know," she said. "I'll see you on Monday."

She headed down the hall, and he closed the door, wondering how he was going to get through the day with no Leila.

Chapter Thirty-one

"No, no, no. This can't be."

Leila looked at the results of the pregnancy test she'd she picked up from Walgreens. She had been in denial for two months but finally couldn't ignore her missed periods. She was carrying Ray's child.

There was no question it was his. She and Devon were just friends, and there was nothing sexual between them. It had to have happened the last time she and Ray were together, just before her world had been thrown out of orbit. How was she going to raise two kids by herself?

"Dear God, no," she cried and sat on the tiled floor in her bathroom. "Shit, shit, shit." She put her face in her hands and sobbed. She cried for what seemed like hours. Her phone rang and snapped her back to reality. It was Devon.

"Hey, beautiful," he said when he answered.

"Hey," she said.

"What's wrong?" he asked.

"Nothing, what's up?"

"Do you want me to get DJ or what? I need to know before I head home."

"Yes, please. I was a little sick today, so I'm at the house and not at the store."

"Lei, I think you should see a doctor. You haven't been feeling well for a while."

"I will tomorrow." *I already know what the problem is.*

"Okay, well, I'll get DJ and keep her tonight. We will see you tomorrow. Feel better," he said, and they hung up.

They were on good footing and were getting along well, and she knew he'd be willing to give her a divorce when they went back to court. She went downstairs and fixed herself a sandwich. Before she could finish eating it, she was throwing up again.

"Damn you, Ray, why did I let you do this to me?" she yelled.

She went to the kitchen and took out a box of crackers. She nibbled on the saltines and debated when and how she would tell him. She wondered if he would even believe her. She finished her snack and went up to her bathroom to take a shower. She looked at the test on the counter again and didn't cringe this time. She thought back to her pregnancy with Deja and how happy she had been. She would be happy with this baby too.

She smiled. "I hope you are a boy, because if you are, you'll be the last one to occupy this space," she said, touching her tummy.

She felt better by the time she got into bed. The next day, she went to the doctor, and he confirmed that she was pregnant. The baby was due in August. She didn't want to tell anyone yet, but she just had to tell Renee.

When there was a lull in customers at the shop, she said, "Well, Renee, Deja's going to be a big sister." She smiled

"What?" Renee's mouth fell open. "You're pregnant?"

"Yep. Dr. Bryce confirmed it this morning. That's why I've been sick every other day."

"My God. How in the hell did you get pregnant? Well, I know how, but I thought you said you and Devon weren't sleeping together."

Leila took a deep breath. "We're not. Ray's the father."

"What? How?" Renee asked.

"The last day we were together, that was the magical day we didn't use any protection." Leila looked away.

"When are you going to tell him?

Leila frowned. Her thoughts had wandered to Ray. "Huh?"

"When are you going to tell Ray?" Renee asked again.

"I have no idea."

Two months later, she still hadn't told him. She knew she had to, but she didn't know how. She was almost five months along and was showing when she and Devon went back in front of the judge. When she told him Devon wasn't the father, he granted her divorce without any more delays. Devon wasn't too happy because he still wanted to work it out, even though he knew he wasn't her baby's father.

By the time she was seven months along, she still hadn't talked to Ray. She still didn't know how. She thought about emailing him, writing him a letter, or even sending him a text message, but none of those options would have been right. And she was terrified to face him.

She was at the store one afternoon and almost fainted when Christa walked in.

"Leila, is that you?" Christa asked. She looked shocked to see Leila.

"Yes, Christa, it's me. How are you?" she asked.

"I've been good. How have you been?" Christa had never been this nice or courteous to her.

"Okay. And pregnant, as you can see." Leila patted her bulging midsection.

"Oh yes, I can definitely see that. How far along are you?"

"Seven and a half months." As soon as she said it, she wished she had lied. She was sure they all knew when she and Ray had broken up.

"I know you haven't spoken to Ray, and I know he has no idea that you are carrying his child," Christa said bluntly. This was the Christa Leila remembered.

"What makes you think it's Ray's child?" Who did Christa think she was?

"Well, thinking back, it was 'bout seven months ago when you guys split, and if Ray had known, he'd be bragging about his first child every day." When Leila didn't say anything, Christa continued. "You really should tell him. He's a good guy," she said.

She wondered why Christa was defending the cheating dog. "So, he's fucking you now?"

"Wow. I never expected to hear something like that from you, but the answer is no. Ray has been my personal trainer for years, and he has always been professional, not only with me but with all of us. The thing is, when you guys broke up, he was devastated behind it, and it took him a long time to get back to normal. He loved you, and I know he'd be there for his child. You not telling him is wrong."

"Do you know what he did to me? He lied to me. And I've tried to tell him. I have."

"You can believe me or not believe me, but the morning that you say he lied to you was a Wednesday. I was there at five a.m., like I am every Wednesday. When I got there, that chick was on the sofa under a beige comforter. That's where she was when I got there and when I left. On my way out, I saw Patricia parking her car. Now if they did it and she got up to get dressed and got on the sofa, hey, I can't say. But I doubt that he slept with her, and I do believe that chick is a liar.

"Two other clients who saw him that day can vouch that she was rude and nasty, and nobody saw him make any kind of personal contact with her. You can continue to keep this from him if you want, but Ray is a good man, and he needs to know. Even if you don't want him back, you need to tell him."

Leila looked at Christa for a moment. Could she trust what she said? "You're sure she was on the sofa?"

"Yes, ma'am. Fully dressed and even had on a pair of boots, if I remember correctly. They were some red boots. I saw them because her feet weren't covered."

"That does make sense." *Who would have sex, get up, get dressed, and go to the sofa?* Leila thought. If Ray wanted to hide her, he would have made her stay in the room so none of his clients could see her.

Christa smiled at her. "I can understand how you felt, but this is a baby."

"You're right. I know I have to tell him, so please don't. Let me," she begged.

"Not a problem. Just don't wait too long, because it looks like you are about to pop," Christa joked. They laughed.

"I know, right?" Leila said.

"Just so you know, I go to Ray three or four times a week, and I have not seen that girl at all. He's not with her," she said.

Leila was happy to hear that. "I believe you, and I'm going to tell him."

"All right. Now show me where the romance novels are, because I need a good one."

"Okay, follow me." Leila helped her find what she needed.

Christa used to be the last bitch she would trust, but she seemed to have changed. Leila thanked God for sending her someone to help her do the right thing.

Chapter Thirty-two

"I know you always tell me to mind my business, Ray, but over the past few months, we have been cool, and I consider you and me to be friends," Christa told him the next morning.

"Okay. Now you know I don't like gossip," he said, helping her with her sit-ups.

"I know, and normally I'd keep my mouth shut, but I saw Leila yesterday."

"Don't. I don't want to hear anything about that woman. I told you months ago to never mention her name to me again," he said. "I've finally gotten to a point where I don't shed tears over her, and I want to stay at this point and move forward."

"This is important. I know you don't wanna hear about her or talk about her, but you really should go by the store to see her."

"No, I shouldn't. Leave it alone."

"It's been months, and I know you're curious to know how she is."

"No, I'm not," he snapped and got up. "Damn, Christa, why did you have to mention that woman's name?"

"You still love her, don't you? I know you do."

"Yes, as much as I hate to admit it, I do," he said and rubbed his head.

"I'm not telling you what to do, but I really think you ought to go and see her."

"Did she ask about me?"

"Yeah, she did, and I know she still loves you. I know you guys miss each other," she said, picking up a towel.

"That may be true, but Leila may not wanna see me."

"Well, it wouldn't hurt to try," she said, nudging his arm.

They finished her workout, and after she left, he thought about Leila for the rest of the day and how nice it would be to see her. He didn't know how smoothly it would go, but he thought it would be good. He decided to take Christa's advice and go see her.

When he got to the store, Leila's truck wasn't there, so he sat in his truck and waited. His cell phone rang, and to his surprise, it was Leila. When he saw her name on the caller ID, he almost dropped the phone trying to answer it.

"Hello," he said. His palms began to sweat.

"Hey," she said. "Is this a bad time?"

"No, no, your timing is perfect."

Leila took a deep breath. "Listen, Ray, I know it's been a long time since we've spoken, and I know you may have moved on and probably aren't interested in talking to me, but I have to talk to you."

"I would love to see you and talk to you," he said. "I mean, I can't believe you're on the other end of this phone. Just say when and where."

She didn't want to see him, but she had to tell him about the baby and before he heard it from someone else. If Christa ran and told him before she got a chance to, it might be a bad thing. Christa hadn't seemed to like her very much before, and although she'd actually been nice the day before, she didn't know if she could trust the woman.

He continued, "Tonight is good. I'm available, and I'd like to see you again."

He's not wasting any time. "Tonight?" she said. "I was thinking this weekend or, you know, next week sometime."

"Next week, huh?" He sounded disappointed.

"It's been a while, and what I have to talk to you about is very important, but I'm so scared to even face you right now."

"There is nothing you can't tell me, no matter how long it's been. I just wanna see you, so whatever it is, it's okay. I'm the one who caused us to break up, and I'm so sorry for allowing Katrina to come in and mess up our good thing. Baby, I swear, even if we never get back together, I did not touch that woman. When I was with you, I was with only you."

Leila was quiet. Tears burned her eyes. If it had not been for Christa telling her what she had seen that morning, she probably still wouldn't have called him.

"Leila, are you there?" he asked.

"Yes, I'm here," she said softly.

"So how about it? Can I see you tonight?"

Leila's stomach got queasy, and his son started to kick as if to say, "Go on, Mom. See him and tell him about me."

She took a deep breath. "Okay."

"Can I come by, or do you wanna come by my place?"

"Your place is fine. I can be there in . . . maybe two hours. I gotta get Deja to Devon, and then I can come by."

"How is Deja? I miss her so much. She was like my little girl, too, you know?"

Leila smiled and rubbed her stomach. He didn't have to pretend anymore, because he had a son on the way. "Yeah, I know," she said. "She's a big girl now. Hopefully you'll see her soon."

"Yeah, I hope so too," he said.

They were quiet for a few seconds, and she cleared her throat. "Listen, Ray, when you see me, I may look a little different. You know, I haven't been working out or eating right since you and I broke up."

"I don't care about any of that. You've always been beautiful. I just wanna see you, all of you, no matter how big or how small. I just wanna see you."

Leila was touched. Rayshon had made her feel beautiful from day one, something Devon had stopped doing as soon as she put on the pounds.

"I'll see you in a little while," she said, pulling into the guest parking stall at Devon's condominium.

"Okay, I'll see you," he said, and they hung up.

She called Devon, and he came down to get Deja. She was asleep, and Leila couldn't carry her anymore. She was two years old now and too heavy for a pregnant woman to be carrying. She told him she was finally going to tell Rayshon about the pregnancy. He wished her luck and gave her a tight hug.

Leila hurried home to shower and get prettied up. It was bad enough she was twenty-five pounds heavier. She couldn't show up looking like a clown. She put on one of her cutest maternity outfits and put on some makeup. She didn't need much because her pregnancy had her skin glowing. Her hair was thick and shiny, also thanks to her pregnancy, and she was glad that she had gone to the salon that afternoon. She stood in the mirror and convinced herself that she could go through with it, then headed out the door.

When she arrived at his complex, she sat in her truck and took a few deep breaths before she got out. She opened the entrance door to his building and contemplated getting back in her truck and going home.

"You can do this," she told herself as she got off the elevator on his floor.

A door opened, and she froze. It was one of Ray's neighbors. She blew out a breath and walked down the hallway to his door before she lost her nerve. She tapped on the door a few times, and she turned her back to it when she heard him unlocking the deadbolt. She was so nervous she thought she'd pass out.

Chapter Thirty-three

"Hey," Ray said.

Leila turned slowly to face him.

"Come on . . ." Words failed him when he saw her stomach.

"I told you I looked different," she said with a small smile.

Ray didn't smile or laugh. She and Devon had obviously gotten back together. There was no chance for them. He swallowed hard and took in her appearance. "Wow," he said. "You're even more beautiful."

"May I come in?" she asked.

"Sure, sure," he said, moving out of her way and letting her inside. He shut the door and offered her a seat. "You definitely look different."

"Yeah, I do," she said. "And I see you are still fine and fit as ever."

"I just focus on work, you know, and going on with my life. I see you've definitely gone on with your life. How far are you? I imagine Devon is happy."

"Well, I am about seven and a half months. Devon wasn't happy at first, but now he's okay with it, I guess. He helps me a lot. We're finally divorced," she said with a smile. "The judge got wind of me carrying another's man child, and he finally granted the divorce."

"Not Devon's, huh?" he asked.

"No," she said. She looked away from him. "Devon isn't the father of my baby."

Ray thought he was going to pass out. They had broken up about seven and a half months ago, and she had gone out, gotten another man that fast, and gotten pregnant. He was outdone.

"Hold on, give me a minute," he said, getting up and going into the kitchen. He grabbed a glass and hit a shot of rum to calm himself. "Do you want anything?" he called to her before he went back into the living room.

"No, I'm good," she said. When he reentered the room, she continued. "This is so hard for me. I wanted to call you so many times, but I was so afraid."

He sat down on the couch. "It's cool. You have a new life, a new man. I can understand."

"Huh?" she asked.

"Your baby. I'm sure you and the father are happy."

"Oooohhhhhhh," she said. "You think I am with someone?" He didn't say anything. "I'm not with anyone. I haven't been with anyone since we broke up."

Ray frowned. How was she pregnant if she hadn't been with anyone else? "Excuse me?" he said, leaning forward.

"Ray, I am carrying your son."

He hopped off the couch. "No fucking way," he said, going back into the kitchen. He grabbed the rum and his glass, took another shot, and decided to bring the bottle and glass into the living room with him.

"I'm so sorry. I didn't want to tell you like this."

"How you gon' come up in here and tell me this shit almost eight months later?" he yelled. She jumped, and he realized he was overreacting. He brought it down a notch. "I'm sorry. I didn't mean to yell," he said, regaining his composure. "I mean, this is just . . ." He stopped abruptly and took another shot of rum. He knew he should lay off the alcohol, but she had just dropped a bomb in his lap.

"I know," she said. "I was just as surprised as you are now."

"You could have told me. I mean, I would have been there for you." He gestured toward her and smiled. "Look at you." He moved closer to her. "Can I?" he asked, wanting to touch her stomach.

"Yes," she said. She took one of his hands and put it on her stomach.

"Oh my God. I can feel him moving. This is real."

"He's been doing somersaults ever since we spoke on the phone earlier."

"How long have you've known he was a boy?"

"Since I was about sixteen weeks."

Ray got on his knees and rubbed her stomach. *This is my baby,* he thought. *Mine.* "Why didn't you tell me?" he asked, looking her in the eye. "I can't understand why you wouldn't tell me." He wanted to hug her and strangle her at the same time.

"I don't know. I was scared and nervous, and I knew if I had been around you and wasn't over you, it would have been more difficult for me. I was heartbroken and confused, and one day turned into another day and then another. Then yesterday, Christa came into the store and we talked, and I begged her to allow me the opportunity to tell you myself."

"So, if you hadn't seen Christa yesterday, you wouldn't have told me?" He turned away from her.

"I've been trying to figure out how to tell you. I don't know when, but I would have told you."

"When?" he yelled. "After my son was born?"

"You know what? You are so right. The conversation we are having right now is the reason why the days continued to go by, and I couldn't tell you." Her eyes watered. "No matter when I told you, I knew you would have reacted this same way, and I was afraid of that."

He got up and walked to the window. "No, you can't say what I would have done, because you didn't give me a choice."

She breathed deeply. "Okay. Now you know, so I'll go." She leaned forward, struggling to get out of the low chair.

Ray rushed over to her. "Wait. I don't want you to go. Sit down and let me get you some water."

He brought her a bottle of water, and she opened it and took a few swallows. They sat quietly for a while. He watched Leila rubbed her stomach and frown.

"Are you okay?" he asked, getting up and moving closer to her.

"He's just doing a dance on me right now. I don't know why he is this excited tonight."

"Maybe it's because he's here in the place where he was conceived." He kneeled in front of her and began rubbing her stomach again. "Do you mind?" he asked, slightly raising the edge of her shirt.

"No," she said.

He lifted her shirt and frowned. *What the hell is she wearing?* The part of the pants that covered her belly was black, and the rest of her pants were green. He slid a finger into the waistband and pulled it outward. The black fabric stretched.

"They're maternity pants, Ray," Leila said, laughing.

"Oh, okay," he said. "I've never seen a pair of pants like this."

Leila pushed the elastic down, exposing her bare belly. It was smooth, and a dark line ran up the middle.

"Wow." He rubbed his hands across her smooth stomach.

"I know. It's huge," she said.

"Yes, it is, but it's beautiful." He couldn't help himself. He leaned forward and planted a soft kiss on the warm skin beneath his hands.

"You know, I never stopped thinking about you for one day," she told him.

"How could you? Every time you look down there's a round reminder of me," he said, and they laughed. It tickled Ray to see how her stomach jumped when she laughed. "I never stopped thinking of you for one minute either, Leila. I do wish you had told me earlier about the baby, but I'm happy that you told me now."

"I am too. I'm so relieved to have finally gotten that out. I feel like I dropped a hundred pounds."

"Well, it looks like you picked up about eighty," he joked, holding her stomach.

She made a face at him. "Ha-ha."

"You know I'm just joking," he said, getting up and reaching for her hand.

"What?" she asked, giving him her hand.

"Come on. I want you to sit with me on the sofa."

He helped her up out of the chair and over to the couch. She sat at one end, and he sat at the opposite end, pulled her feet onto his lap, removed her shoes, and started massaging her bare feet.

Leila sighed and relaxed against a cushion. "Are you seeing anyone?" she asked.

"Nope. I'm still a single man."

"Why is that?"

"I fell in love with this one woman who dropped me cold when she thought I cheated on her. I just could never seem to get over her, so I'm still single. Are you seeing anyone?" After he asked, he remembered she'd said she hadn't been with anyone since their breakup.

"Please, man, look at me. I look like a root beer float. I can't get a man walking around pregnant and swollen."

"I find that hard to believe."

"Be serious."

"I am serious. You're radiant."

"Well, when most men see a pregnant woman, they don't think she's available."

"True," he said and continued to rub her feet. They were quiet for a moment, and then he said, "If I asked, would you be willing to go out with me?"

Leila smiled. "Let's see. I'll have to check my schedule," she said jokingly.

"Oh, it's like that, huh?"

"Nah, I'm kidding. How about you go out with me, let's say . . . tomorrow around three?" she asked.

"Let me see," he said, thinking. "Tomorrow at three, I have Mia, and at four, Jada. How about tomorrow evening?"

"I don't mind tomorrow evening, but I have a doctor's appointment in the afternoon. I thought you'd like to come along and hear the baby's heartbeat and check out his photo shoot."

"Photo shoot?" he asked, puzzled.

"His ultrasound. I've had a slight rise in my blood pressure, and the doctor just wants to take a look to make sure he is fine."

Ray stopped rubbing her feet. "Slight? How slight?"

"Don't worry. I'm fine."

"Your health is a very serious thing. Tomorrow you and I are going for a thirty-minute walk. I'm not taking no for an answer. We can't have your blood pressure high."

"Come on. I get out of breath so easily now. I can't walk for that long."

"We'll walk a pregnant pace. I won't hurt you. I love you, and I want you healthy."

"Okay, I hear you. But what about your appointments?"

"Don't worry about that. Just let me take care of that. And I'll also take care of you and the baby," he said.

Leila smiled. "Ray, I love you too. You just don't know how much I've missed you and how many times I wanted to call or come by. I was so lonely and sad without you."

"We can work our thing out if you want to. We have a baby coming, and my offer still stands."

She cocked her head to one side. "Offer?"

"We were engaged, remember?"

She looked surprised. "You still wanna marry me?"

"Yes, I still wanna marry you. Do you wanna marry me?"

"Yes, Ray, I do," she said, nodding.

"Okay," he said and smiled at her.

"So, where do we go from here?" she asked.

"Well, we can go into the bedroom and do some making up, or we can stay out here and watch TV and talk."

"Option A sounds good," she said.

He laughed. "I figured it would." She sat up, and he helped her stand and led her to the bedroom.

Ray said a prayer of thanks as he helped Leila undress. He hadn't had sex since the last time they were together, and she'd said she hadn't been with anyone since then either. She had joked about her weight gain, but he thought she was perfect. Pregnancy was a good look on her. He made love to her carefully at first, not wanting to hurt her or the baby, but when she moaned and told him she loved him, he gave in to his elation at having her back in his life and the sensation of being inside of her again. They were exhausted when they were done, and they collapsed on top of the covers.

"I see the saying is right. Pregnant pussy is good pussy," Ray joked.

"What?" Leila asked.

"You know, guys say pregnant stuff is the best stuff."

She smiled. "My stuff has always been good."

"No doubt, baby, it has. It was just extra good tonight. I don't know if it has to do with the pregnancy, but damn, I want some more."

"Already?" she asked.

"Yes, ma'am. Need I remind you I haven't had you in almost eight months?"

"Well, I haven't had you either."

"And I am gonna make sure we never have to say those words again."

"You promise?"

"I promise, baby."

Chapter Thirty-four

The next morning, the sound of music woke Leila up. It was a sound she had missed. She smiled, glad to be back in his bed. She eased out of bed and went into the bathroom. When she was done, she looked around the room. It was clean as a whistle, just like she remembered it always being. She went to the vanity to wash her hands and face and saw her toothbrush on the other sink that she used to use. She wondered if it had been there since the breakup. After they broke up, she had never come back to get any of her things.

She went back to the bedroom and checked the dresser drawer that had been hers. Her things were still in there. She wondered where he'd put her baby's playpen and toys. They were going to come in handy for the new baby. She went through the drawer and wondered if she could fit into any of her old clothes. She showered and put on a pair of her old thong

underwear she found in the drawer. The waistband sat underneath her stomach, but otherwise,
they fit okay. She couldn't fit into any of the bras
anymore, so she had to put the same one back
on. She went through Ray's walk-in closet and
found an oversized Chicago Bears jersey and put
it on.

When she finished dressing, she went to the
living room and got her phone out of her purse.
She looked around the room. Her picture wasn't
on the coffee table anymore, but there were a
couple of her and Deja on his mantle and book-
shelves. She walked over and studied them. She
could see the difference in her face from when
she had lost a few pounds and her pregnant face
now.

She looked around the room and smiled. She
couldn't believe she was there. After months of
separation and her being afraid to tell him she
was pregnant, he still wanted to marry her. "You
are too good to be true," she said out loud.

She sat on the sofa, called Renee, and brought
her up to date on what was going on. When
they were done talking, she went to the kitchen.
She opened the fridge and was shocked to see
strawberry cream cheese, the stuff Ray vowed
was no good for her. "Uh-huh, got you hooked
on the creamed cheese, too," she said. She shook

her head and smiled again. She fixed herself a breakfast of fruit and a toasted bagel and sat down on a stool at the island to eat. She heard the music stop. Ray's session was coming to an end.

She couldn't remember who would be there that Wednesday from seven 'til eight, but she recognized the woman's face when she came down.

"Leila, what a surprise. How are you?" she asked with a smile.

Leila stood up. "I'm good, nice to see you again." This was one of Ray's regular clients, but she couldn't remember her name.

"Oh." The woman blinked. "You're having a baby. Ray didn't tell me you guys were back together. And he certainly didn't tell me about your little bundle."

"Yes, well, our son will be arriving soon," Leila said, correcting her. He was not her bundle. He was their bundle.

"Ray's going to be a dad? Get out. No way." she said.

Leila wondered if that meant, "Stop yo' lying. That ain't his baby."

"Yes, Rayshon is going to be a daddy," she said.

Just then, Ray came down the steps. "Good morning. How did you sleep?" he asked her. He kissed her on the forehead.

"Amazing. I didn't realize how much I missed that bed." Too late, she realized the woman was still standing there. *Patricia, that's her name,* she suddenly remembered.

"Well, congratulations to you both," Patricia said, walking to the door.

"Thank you, Patricia," Leila said.

"Yeah, thanks," Ray said. "I'll see you on Saturday." He shut the door behind her. "I have two more clients, and then I'm all yours," he said, walking over to Leila.

"It's only eight in the morning. How did you manage that?"

"I rescheduled all my afternoon appointments."

"All of them? Impossible," she said. Ray was a busy man. He almost always had back-to-back appointments.

"My people are cool. Once I told them that I had to go with you for an ultrasound, they said no problem." He moved closer to her and pulled her into an embrace. "Now I'll be done in time for us to take a nice walk in the park and still make it to the doctor on time."

She chuckled and shook her head. He lifted her chin to kiss her, but there was a knock on the door before their lips touched.

"Duty calls," Leila said and smiled as he went to the door.

"Angela," he said, "come on in."

"Hey, Ray, what's—" She stopped when she saw Leila.

"Hi, Angela," Leila said with a smile.

"Leila. My God, you're huge," she said.

Leila sighed and looked up at the ceiling. "I'm pregnant, Angela," she said. The space ball was a size zero in the brains as well.

"Oh, I was gon' say," Angela said.

Leila couldn't help but laugh. The poor girl was slow, Leila thought.

"Babe, I'll see you shortly," Ray said and gave her a quick kiss before he and Angela went upstairs.

"Did she tell you that was yo' kid?" she heard Angela ask in a low voice.

"It is my child, Angela. And for the hundredth time, my personal business is not your business. Now let's get started."

Leila shook her head and went back to Ray's room. Just as she walked in, the phone rang. She thought back to Katrina answering his phone and decided not to do that. When his answering machine beeped for the caller to leave a message, she heard Katrina's voice. She was tempted to snatch the phone off the hook, but she just listened.

"Rayshon, this is Kat again. I've left you thousands of messages, and I've come by and left you notes. Like I said, the past is the past, and it's time you forgive me and give me a chance. I'm sorry for lying to Leila. I don't know how to make you see. I did it because I love you. Again, please call me. It's been months. You can't still be mad." The call ended, and the machine beeped.

Leila looked down at the flashing number on the machine. Ray had twenty-one messages. She wondered if he had listened to any of them but figured he hadn't, since all had been left over the previous two days. She tried to resist but gave in and hit the play button. Of the twenty-one messages, three were telemarketers. The other eighteen were from Katrina. She listened to Ray's ex breathe on the line until the machine cut her off. She listened to her cry, and she listened to her angry "I hate you" messages. How could someone be hooked for so long on someone who refused to even talk to them? Love was love, she thought. After all this time not talking to Ray, she still loved him, and he still loved her. She felt kind of sorry for Katrina, but she also felt that the bitch got what she deserved.

One thing that made her feel better was the reassurance the messages gave her. Katrina had confirmed that Rayshon made no efforts to see or talk to her since telling Leila she and Ray were getting back together. That made her feel like shit for treating Ray so horribly. Tears welled in her eyes when she thought about how much time they had lost and couldn't get back. She regretted not telling him about the baby sooner.

She put her hands on her stomach and told her baby that she was sorry and that she made a mistake. She told him that, from then on, she would never keep anything away from his father, and she was going to do her part to make things perfect for all of them.

She wiped her eyes and, although she knew it was inappropriate, hit the button to delete all the messages on his machine. Then she grabbed the remote, got into bed, turned on the TV, and waited for Ray to finish.

After he saw his last client out, he came into the bedroom and started to undress.

Leila muted the TV. "Katrina called," she told him.

He paused and looked at Leila. "I don't talk to her, Lei," he said.

"I know," she said and smiled. "I just wanted to tell you something. Come here and sit," she said, sitting up in the bed. He sat down next to her. "I'm sorry for not believing you when you told me the truth. I'm sorry for walking out on you and for not telling you about the baby sooner."

"Leila, baby—"

"No, please hear me out. We've lost so much time. I should have trusted you. I was so angry, and I didn't believe that I was special enough for someone to love me. I had a horrible self-image, and it was easy to accept that you wanted the sexy, petite, head-turning Katrina over me. I didn't stop and see that looks had nothing to do with it. You gave back what Devon took from me. You treated me like I was more beautiful than Christa, Mia, Veronica, and all those other stunning women you work with, and you never once acted like you were ashamed to be with the big girl. I'm sorry for not having faith in what we had and letting a chick like Katrina's ugly ass come between us. No matter how pretty and petite she is, she has ugly ways, and that makes her, in my opinion, an ugly person."

She took a deep breath. "I listened to all the messages that she left. And I deleted them, too. I trust you. And I know that if no other man sees me as beautiful, you do. I thank you for what you did for me back then, and I thank you for holding on to me in your heart. You are my match, and I see now that we are made for each other. I love you."

Ray touched her face. "We're going to be okay. We have a new baby coming, and we have a promising future. I am going to see to it that nothing like that ever happens again. I'm sorry, too, for putting myself in a situation like I did with Kat. You had every right to feel like you felt, because it did look pretty bad. I still, to this day, sometimes wonder what possessed that crazy-ass girl to stuff her panties between my mattress and headboard," he said, and they laughed. "But seriously, it doesn't matter where we were then. All that matters is that I have you now." He pulled her close and kissed her passionately.

"You trying to get some?" she asked when he tugged on the jersey.

"Oh yes, and if you give me some, we don't have to do that walk." He stood and took off his sweats, revealing his beautiful erection.

Leila licked her lips. "Oh, you don't have to ask me twice," she said, taking off the jersey.

After, she wondered how in the hell she had lasted this long without him.

Chapter Thirty-five

Despite what he'd said earlier, Ray still talked Leila into going for a walk in the park. They held hands, and Leila thought heaven had come down to earth for her. They sat on the bench for a little while before going to her appointment.

"Leila, I'm so happy that we are here at this moment. This day . . . I mean, it's beautiful. You are beautiful, and this is just so perfect. I hate I missed out on everything."

"You didn't miss much. I mean, we still have weeks before he comes," she said, holding her belly.

"I did. The first doctor's appointment, the five-minute wait while the test processes, the cravings, the sickness."

"The cravings are still here, trust me. I wish I had a bagel with strawberry cream cheese right now. And the sickness I occasionally have, but not often," she said, making a face. "If you want that stick test, we can run to Walgreen's, grab one, and you can watch it turn blue." They laughed.

"You're too much, you know that?" Ray said.

"No, baby, you take the cake," she said.

"We better get going," he said, standing and reaching for her.

"Hey, you're right, we wanna be on time."

"Yes, we do, sexy momma. All this belly and you are still sexy," he said, putting an arm around her after helping her up.

"I'm huge, babe."

"And still gorgeous to me."

She smiled. "You are so amazing. Can you please always love me?" she said.

"I can do that," he said

Ray sat on a hard, plastic chair, nervous as the nurse checked Leila's vitals. Her blood pressure was normal. He shook a little when the doctor came in and got ready to do the exam.

"Hello, Leila," Dr. Bryce said. "How are you feeling?"

"I'm perfect," she responded, looking at Ray. He smiled at her.

"I'm happy to see that your pressure is normal, and I am thrilled to see who I think I can safely assume is the reason for the smile on your face."

The doctor turned on the sink and washed his hands. "You must be Rayshon Sr.?" he asked Ray.

"Yes, I am," Ray said nervously.

"Ever since Leila found out she was carrying a boy, we've all known him as Rayshon Jr.," Dr. Bryce said.

"Well, I'm very anxious to meet my son too," Ray said. He reached over and held Leila's hand.

"I'll let you guys listen to his heartbeat first and, Leila, I know your pressure looks good today, but I'm going to do that ultrasound anyway just to be absolutely sure he is doing well."

Dr. Bryce pulled the bottom of her shirt up, exposing Leila's swollen belly. Ray watched as he took the gel from a warmer and squeezed it in a small spot on her stomach. Then he picked up a handheld device and put it in the gel. The room filled with the sound of a heartbeat. Ray's breath caught, and tears ran down his cheeks. This was his son's heartbeat. He swallowed hard and looked at Leila. "His heartbeat sounds good and strong," Dr. Bryce said.

A nurse came in, and they set up for the ultrasound.

By the time they turned on the lights, Ray was speechless. The doctor had pointed out all of the baby's organs and his genitals. He had never seen anything so amazing in his life.

"It shouldn't be too much longer," Dr. Bryce said. "Everything looks great. I want you to go home and take it easy. Enjoy the next few weeks, and on August nineteenth, we should see this little one in person." He turned to Ray. "It was nice to meet you, Mr. Johnson. I'm sure you played a part in helping improve my patient's blood pressure. Please take care of her and the baby for me."

Ray shook his hand and smiled. "Don't worry. I will take care of them," he said.

The doctor left, Ray helped Leila off the table, and they headed out. They got into his truck, and he started it and pulled out of the parking lot. They rode in silence.

"Leila, baby, let's get married," Ray said suddenly.

She looked at him blankly. "Huh?" she asked.

"Married. Let's just do it."

"Are you serious?"

"Yes, let's get married right now. I don't want to go another day without you being my wife."

"Rayshon, are you crazy? I mean, we live in separate houses and . . . I mean, we just can't get married right now."

"I don't care about us living in two separate houses. That's a small issue that we can work out easily." He took her hand. "I want to marry you today. I don't want to wait."

"We have to get a license, and we have to think about the house and the loft and Deja."

"Do you love me?"

"Yes," she said.

"Do you want me?" he asked, pulling over and parking.

"Of course I do," she said.

"Then there isn't one reason for us not to do this. I love you, and I want my son to be born with his parents being married."

"Okay, baby, let's get married," she said.

Ray kissed her and drove them to the courthouse. They applied for the license and had to wait three days before they could actually get married. The following week, they were married, and Leila's house and Ray's loft were on the market. They knew it would be tight, but they managed to find a house the next week and put in a contract on it. Three mortgages would be a stretch for them, but they were ready to do whatever it took to be under the same roof.

Leila was getting bigger, and it was getting harder for her to move around, so she was at Ray's loft most of the time. She was two weeks from her due date, and she still hadn't told Devon that she and Ray were married. He knew the house was on the market, but he didn't know she was selling it because they were already married.

On a visit to pick Deja up, Devon stayed awhile to visit, something he usually did.

"Lei, let me see your hand," he asked suddenly.

"Huh?" she said like she didn't hear him.

"Is that a band in front of your engagement ring?" he asked.

"Yes," she said and looked away.

"What's going on?"

"I'm married, Devon. Ray and I got married three weeks ago," she confessed.

"What? You fucking got married behind my back?"

"No, I got married and didn't tell you," she said.

"Why? Why didn't you tell me?" he asked.

"I didn't want to hurt you. You were upset with me when you found out I was pregnant with Ray's baby, and I thought you'd be upset with me getting married."

"Listen, we are divorced. You are damn near nine months pregnant, and I know you love him. You didn't have to keep that from me."

"You're right. I wanted to tell you, but I didn't know how. So there it is. I'm married, and I'm happy." She tried to walk off, but he grabbed her hand.

"I'm glad you're happy. I am happy for you. You will always have a place in my heart, and

I will forever be here for you and Deja." He pointed to her stomach. "And this little stranger, too, if you need me to be."

Leila hugged him. "Thanks, Devon. Thank you so much. I'm so happy to have you in my life as a friend. You have truly been a good friend to me, and I know it wasn't easy. It took a lot for either one of us to get to this point."

Ray walked in. "Hello, Devon," he said, putting the bags he carried on the island. "I got your favorite from the Chinese spot," he told Leila.

"Thanks, baby," she said, looking in the bag. "I'm going to be right back. I gotta grab some of DJ's things for Devon."

She went upstairs, leaving the men alone in the kitchen.

"Congratulations, man," Devon said.

"Lei finally told you?" Ray asked, taking the food from the bags.

"Yeah. I had to ask, but she told me."

"I told her a hundred times to tell you, but you know Leila. She does things when she is ready."

"Yeah, I know her. Listen, Ray, we have two of the same women in common, and I trust that you will do your part to make sure they stay happy," Devon said.

"I got you covered," Ray said. "Just keep in mind that we're family. My son will be in your

life, too, so we have to be good men and be good
fathers and respect Leila as the mother of our
children at all times."

"I got you," Devon said, and they shook hands.
"When you want to hang out and do what dads
do with their kids, let me know."

Both men turned when they heard Leila come
down the stairs. Deja was right behind her.

"Here you go, Devon," she said. "I'll get her
this weekend, and if you need me, don't hesitate
to call." She kissed Deja.

"We're good. You take it easy, Ray," he said.

"You too," Ray said. "And hold on. I got to get
my sugar too before DJ bounces. Give me a hug,
li'l momma." Deja hugged him and kissed his
cheek. "See you later, big girl," he said.

"See you later, gator," Deja said and grabbed
her daddy's hand. "Come on, Daddy, let's go
bye-bye."

"Bye, sweetie pie," Leila said.

"Bye-bye, Mommy," she said.

Chapter Thirty-six

Leila was enjoying life. The baby was born, they were in their new home, her old house had sold, and Ray's loft had finally gone under contract. He had kept doing training sessions there until after Leila's house sold, and then they were able to rent a space a few blocks from her bookstore. He had decided to start with a small gym until he was able to open a full-sized spot. All of his clients moved with him to his new location, and his business was doing well due to word of mouth. It was scary for both of them, but they did it. Devon and Ray were cool, and he and Leila had a true friendship that Leila never thought would happen. They were closer divorced than they had been when they were married.

The weather was getting cold, and Leila was glad that they had all the major moving and hard work out of the way. They were at Ray's loft, getting the last few boxes. Leila was in her truck, waiting for Ray to come down. She noticed a car pull into a parking space across the street. As she watched, a petite woman got out and walked across the street past Leila's truck and went toward the building. The car and the woman were vaguely familiar. The woman's identity hit her just as the woman disappeared into the building. It was Katrina.

"Aw naw, bitch, not today," Leila said, turning off the engine and getting out of the truck.

The elevator doors closed before Leila reached it, so she had to wait for the next car. When she finally got to his floor, she exited the elevator and went to the front door. It was partially open, and she could see Katrina and hear her voice. She stopped and listened.

"What's going on, Ray?" Katrina said. "You trying to move on me? I've tried calling, and when your phone said, 'No longer in service,' I had to make sure you were okay."

"You got a lot of nerve coming over here," Ray said. Leila couldn't see him from where she stood, but she could hear him clearly.

"What'd you expect? You never returned any of my calls and then no service on your phone. What was I supposed to do?"

"Stay away. I expected you to stay the fuck away. I don't have time for you. I'm on my way out. I'm married now, and my wife would mop the floor with your ass if she knew you were here." He moved farther into the room, and Leila could see him. He set a box he was carrying on to the floor and crossed his arms.

"You married that fat bitch?" Katrina snapped.

"Leila. Yes, I married Leila, and we have a beautiful son. You know what? Let me call my wife to come up. She's right downstairs." He reached into his pocket.

Leila pushed the door the rest of the way open and walked in. "You don't have to call me, baby. I'm right here."

Katrina whirled around. Her ankle-length coat hung open, and Leila took in the skintight jeans and body-hugging, low-cut sweater. "L . . . Leila," Katrina stammered. "Uh, hi. I was, um, in the neighborhood and I, um . . ."

Leila held her hands up. "Save the shit. I hope this will be the last time we see your trifling ass again. The 'fat bitch' has had it with you fucking with her man. Now I hope I'm not going to ever have to tell you again to stay the fuck away from my husband." She stepped close to Katrina. "If I ever do have to tell you again, I will mop the floor with ya bony ass. You got that?"

Ray stepped between the two women. "Kat, you may wanna bounce," he said, putting his arms around Leila. They watched her run out the front door as if the building were on fire. "Damn, baby," he told Leila, "calm down. You're a mother." He kissed her.

"And a jealous wife. I'm not having it with these bitches. They are going to feel the wrath of this big girl if they keep coming at my man."

"I see. I bet we won't be seeing Katrina's ass again."

"Oh, I know we won't," she said.

Devon released her and picked the box up. "Okay, Mayweather, let's go so we can get our kids."

Leila followed him out. "Okay. And after that, I'm in the mood for Chinese," she said and shut the door.

The End

Here's a sneak peek . . .

Now You Wanna

Come Back 2

Chapter One

Leila stood in the front of her empty store, glaring out the window and holding her stomach. She was pregnant with baby number three and wondered how she could be losing her store in the middle of what was supposed to be the best moment of her life. Rayshon managed to have a booming business and was opening his third location, but ebooks had been the downfall to her store's success. After four years of so-called making it through the depression, recession, or whatever society was calling folks having no money nowadays, she wondered how electronic books had grown so fast.

"Damn, won't they miss the smell of the pages? Now people have to plug in their books, ain't that some shit," she said, shaking her head, thinking about the Kindle Rayshon had gotten her for her birthday that year, which was still in its box. "What would really piss me off is to get to the climax of my book and my battery die and have no place to plug in. I would wanna punch somebody, that's for damn sure," she said out loud, watching the shippers load the last boxes of her books onto the truck. "Damn, damn, damn, this is all I ever wanted, and now I have to wait for online orders. Shit!" she said, and walked over to the counter and picked up her phone.

She knew Rayshon was not available, but she called him anyway. "Hey, it's me. I just wanted to tell you I'll meet you at the house for dinner. I hope you can make it this time. My day has been hell, and your daughter has kicked a couple of field goals in my belly, and I don't want to put RJ to bed alone tonight," she said and hung up.

She looked around, and her eyes burned with tears, but she blinked them back. "All is not lost. My online bookstore has got to bring in some profit," she told herself and did a quick walk through of her now-empty space. It was still hers until the space sold, and she prayed that that wouldn't take forever, because she had no other uses for it and she was fresh out of ideas.

"We are headed to the storage, Mrs. Johnson," the driver said, and she nodded.

"Okay, Chad, you know that everything is labeled. Please inform your workers to place the boxes in their appropriate spaces that are labeled in my storage. As you can see, I am not in any shape to be moving boxes around," she said, holding her tummy. She was a week away from being eight months, and this little girl in her womb was a kicker.

"No worries, Mrs. Johnson, we will take care of everything. By the way, I am sorry to see your store closing. My wife only comes to your store for her books, and she is torn up too," he expressed, and Leila was touched.

"Thanks. Just let her know that she can still order online at my website. Leila's Books will still be available online until I'm sold out," she said with a smile. Behind her smile was a frown, but she didn't want to show emotion.

"Will do," Chad said and walked out the door.

Leila stood there and looked around and wondered if she should try something else with the space, but nothing came to mind quickly enough for her to feel better or excited. She grabbed her purse and keys and took one last look before she turned out the lights. She locked the door and headed for her truck. Her Armada was paid in full, and even though Rayshon insisted she get a newer one, she refused. She drove a few blocks down to Rayshon's gym and hoped that he was there. He had just opened a new location, and she was relieved that folks cared enough about their bodies to make him a successful business owner, since no one cared about reading books with real pages anymore.

While her business declined, her husband's business inclined. In four years, his business skyrocketed and hers sank deeper and deeper into the ground. Leila congratulated Rayshon, but deep down she didn't like that she was going nowhere and he was pulling business in like a magnet. There would be days when she didn't even have to open because she'd get only one or two customers, and the first question they would ask after confirming the book was in stock was, "Is it available on Kindle?" Kindle became a name that Leila despised, and she wanted to punch Rayshon in the throat when he gave her hers.

"No more featured authors. No more visits with the famous authors I welcomed who had a line around the corner. No more book release parties. God, I'm going to miss my store," she said to herself as she parked in the employee-only parking area. She was sad not to see her husband's Denali, but she parked anyway, just to go inside to check on things.

She walked past the front desk and gave a couple brief hellos and made her way back to what used to be Rayshon's main office. His new manager, Ankwan, was on the phone, smiling like he was engaged in a call that was not business related. "Hey, look, babe, I'll hit you back," he said and quickly hung up the phone. "Leila, what brings you by?" he asked like he wasn't too happy to see her.

"Do I need a reason?" she asked and put her purse on the desk.

"Naw, I was just wondering. Ray hasn't been by here in days, and you popping in is like rare."

"Well, as you know, my store closed today, and since I'm less than a mile away, I decided to drop in," she said, rubbing her tender belly. It was so sore from the abuse that was going on from kung fu master, "get me the hell up outta here" baby number three.

"Yeah, I heard, and I'm sorry. Ray told us in our last staff meeting."

"Oh, okay," she said with a fake smile. "I was just in the neighborhood, and I thought maybe Ray would be at this location, but I see he is not," she said, grabbing her purse. "I'll let you get back to business," she said, and turned to walk out, and Ankwan didn't stop her. She knew he was anxious to call back whomever he was talking to.

Leila got into her truck and called Ray again, and she got his voicemail. She hung up without leaving a message, and then she called Devon.

"Hey, Lei," he answered on the second ring.

"Hey, it's me, Lei," she said.

"I know. I just said, 'Hey, Lei,'" he laughed lightly. "What's up?"

"Ummm, I know this is last minute, but since this is your weekend with DJ, do you think you can keep RJ tonight too? I had a really hard day with the store closing, and I need a mommy break."

"Sure, that's not a problem, but you know how Ray gets when RJ stays with me overnight."

"I know, but Ray keeps these long hours now. You know, with the third gym opening, he is hardly home to help me, and my stomach is so, so sore, and I just can't do it tonight. By the time Ray gets home, he won't even realize that they are both gone."

"Okay. No worries, and I'm sorry about the store. I know how much that place meant to you. And so what if Ray is opening his third gym? He should be at home helping you. I know this pregnancy is hard for you, and I wish I could be there to help you," he said.

"Come on, Devon, don't. Ray is a good man and a good husband and a great dad. He's just been swamped, so don't."

"I know, and I didn't mean anything by it. I am not trying to upset you. I will get the kids and give you a break. What time will you guys be home?"

"In an hour or so. Deja is already home with Ta, and as soon as I get off with you, I am going to call her to get their overnight bags packed. I'm on my way to pick up li'l Ray now," she said and paused. "Are you sure? I'm not interfering with any of your plans with her, am I?"

"It's my weekend to get DJ, so I have no plans with her tonight, but tomorrow, you must get RJ by five because Deja and I have a date."

"No problem, Mr. Vampelt. I wouldn't dare ruin my daughter's date," she said with a smile. She and Devon were like best friends now, and he was the best father on the planet when it came to Deja. Even though she and Rayshon did well financially, Devon paid child support to the max and still did all the extras without complaint.

"I'll see you in an hour. Make sure you pack DJ's swimsuit because she is going to need it," he said, and Leila just smiled.

"I will, but you know I need you to keep an eye on her in that water. She thinks she is Flipper and tries to dive in the deep end," she said and pulled into the daycare parking lot. She was so happy that RJ would be going to school the next year, because she was tired of paying daycare.

"I got this."

"I know, babe," she said and caught herself. "I mean, Devon. I know," she said and hung up. She went inside and picked up her son, and then she headed home.

"Hey, Mrs. J. Deja has eaten, and li'l Ray's dinner is in the warmer. I cleaned everything in the kitchen, and the kids' bags for their sleepover with Mr. Vampelt are by the door."

"Thanks, Tabitha, but one last thing. I'm going to need you to grab Deja's swimsuit, please. I forgot to tell you to pack it," she said, and Tabitha dashed to Deja's room without dispute. Leila knew she had something going on or somewhere to be, because she was short in conversation and exited the room too quickly. "Hey, DJ, your dad will be here shortly to pick you guys up."

"You guys? I thought it was going to be my daddy and me this weekend."

"RJ is gonna tag along for one night to give Mommy a li'l me time."

"Why can't Daddy Ray keep RJ for your me time?" she asked, and Leila was about to explain, but Tabitha walked back into the kitchen.

"Deja's swimsuit is all packed. Is there anything else, Mrs. Johnson?"

"Umm, no, we are good. Enjoy your weekend," Leila said, and Tabitha kissed the kids goodbye and promptly made her exit. Devon arrived not too long after, and Leila was all alone. She looked to see what Tabitha cooked and frowned at the ground beef and pasta cheese dish that was in the pot. She grabbed a bowl to put it in, and she washed the pot and put it away. She made her way up the stairs and exhaled.

The beautiful three-level home that she and Rayshon purchased was so lonely lately because he was never home. She took a shower and sat in her baby's nursery. "Things are supposed to be better, Ray. You promised me that things would be great, but they are not," she said, rubbing her belly. "How did we create this distance? No, how did you create this distance?" she asked aloud and then dozed off in her rocker. Things were perfect before work came before their marriage. Ray was her comfort, but now she had to comfort herself.

The countdown to the closing day of her store approached quickly, and every day Rayshon treated it as if it were no big deal. "Don't worry. This will give you more time with the kids and time to enjoy your pregnancy," was all he'd say, and she couldn't believe that he took it so lightly. Her dream was now a nightmare, and she was starting to feel like she was in her marriage all alone.

Chapter Two

"I think I need to see something a little bigger," Ray told Kennedy, and she put the two-carat diamond pendant back. "My wife has had a terrible week, and I want to put a smile on her face for a change," Ray told her.

"I see," Kennedy said. "I know exactly what would make a woman feel better. Can I show you something other than a necklace?" she asked, and Ray was open for suggestions.

"Sure. I just want to cheer her up," he said and followed Kennedy over a couple cases from where they were.

"Now this," she said, showing him a beautiful tennis bracelet, "would definitely put a smile on my face if I were having a bad week."

"Yes, it's beautiful, but I don't know," he said because Leila had a tennis bracelet similar to that one already. "You're the owner of this store, aren't you?"

"Yes, I am," Kennedy said with pride.

"Show me something that would help to ease your pain if your store went outta business," he said, and Kennedy then showed him to another case.

"Teresa, can you get Mr. Johnson a glass of champagne, and we will find a gift suitable enough to cheer up his wife who just lost her business?" Kennedy said. "Now this is what we call our high rollers case. Anything from this case would make the saddest person happy."

"Let's see what you got," Rayshon said. He took the glass of champagne that the other young lady handed him, and then he took a sip. "Wow, this is good."

"Thank you. We just recently added a refreshment station to my store, and customers now come in just for a drink and a snack." Kennedy laughed lightly as she unlocked the case. She reached in and grabbed a pair of earrings. "These are one of our popular items," Kennedy said and went on to give Rayshon more details about them. After Kennedy showed Rayshon a couple more items, he asked to see a diamond necklace, and Kennedy smiled. "This one is one of my favorite pieces. This would definitely make a woman not only feel better but want to reward you." She winked.

Rayshon admired it. "This is lovely, and I know Leila will love this."

"Leila, Leila. I know Leila is a sorta common name, but I know a Leila who just went out of business. Your wife isn't from Leila's Books, is she?" Kennedy asked, and he was surprised she knew of his wife's store.

"Yes. Today was the last day of business for her."

"I'm so sorry. I've been going to her store for a couple of years. My husband has a restaurant not even a block down from her store."

"Small world. The owner of the restaurant, your husband, Julian, is a member at my fitness center down the street."

"Shut up, you're Mr. Johnson of Johnson Physicals?"

"Yes, I am."

"I heard you just opened your third location," she said, and Ray took a sip of his drink.

"While my business is growing through the roof, my wife's didn't hold on this year," he said sadly.

"Tell Leila that I am deeply sorry. This place is my baby, and even though we have a couple restaurants and nightclubs, I still love this store, so I can't imagine how she is feeling."

"That is exactly why you have to gift wrap this lovely necklace for me, so I can try to cheer her up. Opening my third location has had me swamped, and I work so many hours I know my wife thinks I am the worst guy on the planet, but I am not. I honestly hate that she had to give up the store, and it kills me that I am having so much success. I can't even look at her. I don't know what to say to make her feel better, and she is pregnant with our third child, and I don't want her stressing. So to keep my sanity, I work. I move around."

"I can't tell you how to handle your marriage, but I will tell you that working and avoiding her isn't going to make her feel better. Even if you just hold her hand, just show her that you wanna be there for her."

"Yeah," he said, and he nodded in agreement. He was so used to being able to cheer Leila up, but with this one, it was hard because she made him feel bad at times for his business being such a success.

"You finish your champagne, and I'll have this wrapped right away for you," she said and moved to the back to have Tiffany gift wrap it for her.

Gift in hand, Rayshon left the jewelry store and headed to the flower shop. He looked down at his phone and saw he had missed a couple calls from Leila, so he listened to her voicemails. He was anxious to get home that night because he hadn't had dinner with his family in weeks.

When he walked through the door, he was surprised that the house was so quiet. He went into the kitchen and was a little disappointed because there were no pots on the stove and he didn't see any takeout. He put the flowers and his briefcase on the kitchen island and removed Leila's gift-wrapped present from the KBanks Jewelers bag, grabbed her flowers, and walked up the stairs to find her. He went into the master first, and there was no sight of her. Then he stuck his head into his son's room, thinking she'd be there with RJ, but she wasn't there either. He knew Deja should have been with Devon, but he looked in her room anyway, and he wondered where they were with Leila's truck parked in the garage.

He stood in the hall and noticed the light coming from the baby's room, and he knew that's where she was. He gently pushed the door open to find Leila sleeping peacefully in her rocker, and he approached slowly to keep from scaring her. He leaned in and kissed her forehead, and she opened her eyes, and he smiled.

"When did you get home?" she asked.

"A couple moments ago. How are you feeling? Where is RJ?" he asked, and she rubbed her face as if she needed help waking up.

"Umm, RJ went to Devon's with Deja," she said.

"Where did he take them?"

"Home. I wasn't feeling well, so Devon agreed to take him overnight for me to get some rest, and please don't make a big deal of it, okay? I know you don't like RJ staying the night."

"So why did you allow him to go overnight?" he asked with a little irritation in his tone.

"Because you have been working every weekend and staying out past his bedtime a lot lately, and I needed a physical and mental break from him," she expressed, getting up from the rocker.

He changed his tone. "Listen, it's fine, okay?" he said. He wanted to cheer her up and not make her upset. "And these are for you," he said, handing her the flowers, and he kissed her. "And this is also for you," he said, handing her the gift.

"What's this?" she asked, setting the flowers on the baby's changing table.

"This is a little something to say that I love you and I am proud of you, and I am sorry your store closed," he said, and tears welled in her eyes. She slowly opened the pretty package and gasped when she saw the beautiful necklace.

"Oh, Ray, this is lovely. This is beautiful." She smiled, admiring it.

"You like it?" he asked, happy.

"Like it? I love it, but I have to pee," she said and handed him the box. She hurried down the hall, and he grabbed the flowers and followed her.

"I'm gonna head downstairs," he said, and she yelled, "Okay," from the bathroom. He went down into the kitchen and grabbed the vase for the flowers. She joined him within minutes.

"The necklace is beautiful, babe, thank you," she said, and he walked over to her and embraced her.

"I'm glad you like it. And the saleswoman knows you. Her name is Kennedy Roberson."

"I know her. She was one of my loyal customers. Her husband owns the restaurant on the corner."

"Yes, Julian. He is also a member of the gym."

"I know, she told me back when she was pregnant with her twins. She swore she'd join too after she had the babies, but I guess things change."

"Yep, sometimes they do," he said and moved over to the wine cooler.

"God, I wish I could have that right now," Leila said, and her eyes watered.

"You can. You know one glass won't hurt."

"I know, but the way I feel, I want to have the entire bottle," she said, wiping her tears.

"Aw, come on, Lei. We've talked about this and talked about it. It's not the end of the world."

"That's easy for you to say because your dream of owning a gym has come true. And not only do you own one, you own three, and my one and only bookstore is closed," she pouted and leaned back against the counter and touched her stomach. "This little girl is abusing this one spot right here, and I want to just scream," she sobbed. She frowned, holding that one spot. Ray rushed over to her side.

"Why are you getting upset about this all over again? Come on and sit down. You are getting worked up, and you know it's not good for you or the baby," he said, and she followed him into the family room. She sat on the couch, and he sat in front of her on the coffee table. "I keep telling you that I will take care of us. You can be a full-time mom to our children and relax and take care of us now, without Tabitha," he said again for the hundredth time.

"Don't give me that same old 'what I can do now.' Are you not hearing me? I loved my store. I love being around my books and getting up every day servicing customers in my own store. That meant so much to me, and I don't have that anymore. I loved having authors visit and read from their novels and having release parties, and that is gone."

"What do I mean to you? What do the kids mean to you?" he asked, and she stood up.

"You know what? Thank you for the flowers and the necklace," she said, walking away.

"Where are you going?" he yelled behind her.

"To Christa's," she said, slipping her swollen feet into her flip-flops.

"Why? I came home early to be with you and to make you feel better, not for you to run out on our conversation."

"I never thought there would come a day in this marriage that you would not understand me," she said, moving swiftly, looking for her keys.

"What? What are you talking about? You're acting as if the world has come to an end because your bookstore closed when you have so many other things to be grateful for," he said, and she nodded at him.

"I know what I have, and I am grateful, but what you fail to realize is that the bookstore was a part of my life. Not more important than you and the kids, but just as important, and I lost it, and if I cry too much or bother you with my loss, I'm sorry!" she yelled and walked out the door, slamming it as hard as she could.

Ray banged his fist on the table, wondering how this turned into such a horrible night when he was only trying to make things right.

Chapter Three

"Hold on, Devon," Christa said, getting up from the sofa. "Someone is at the door," she said and walked over to the peephole. "It's Leila. Let me call you back," she said and ended the call. She opened the door and could tell she had been crying. "Leila, what's wrong? Come in," she said and shut the door.

"I need to talk, but first the bathroom," she said, and Christa nodded. Over the years, she and Leila had grown close, and now that she and Devon were seeing each other, they saw each other even more. Christa went into the kitchen and grabbed a couple bottles of water from the fridge and sat on the sofa to wait for Leila to return.

"I'm sorry to come by so late, but Devon has the kids, and I'm trying to get away from them right now. I don't need my kids to see me cry another day, you know," she said with one hand on her head and the other placed on her belly.

"Come on, Leila, sit," Christa instructed, handing her a bottle of water. Leila took it and flopped down onto the sofa and let out a huff.

"I just feel . . . I dunno," she said, and another tear fell.

"Relax, girl. Take a deep breath and tell me what's going on," she said, and Leila looked at her like her life was falling apart.

"All I can think about is my bookstore, and all Ray has for me is how great it will be for me to become this supermom and wife. I love my family, Christa, you know that. I love my man, and my kids are my world, but do you know how good it felt to open my bookstore? As bad as my marriage was with Devon, he was behind me a hundred ten percent when I decided to open my store." She paused and took a gulp of her water. She took a few deep breaths and continued, "And now, all that work is just down the drain."

"I understand, but you can't stress and dwell on it. You are going to be okay without the store. You didn't fail, and at least you got to do something you wanted to do. Not all people can say that."

"I know, but what if your agent called you tomorrow and said your modeling career is over and nobody wants you to model their clothes, makeup, or shoes, or see that beautiful smile on a billboard?" she said, and Christa looked down and didn't say anything. "Exactly. See, that's how I feel. I know I am a good mother and a great wife, and I was that when I had my bookstore."

"You have to get out of this rut. I hear you. It would absolutely kill me if I got that call, but I would be able to say that I did what I set out to do, and so can you. You can do other things. This doesn't mean life is over," she said.

"It's just going to take some time to get over it," she said and swallowed more Evian. They sat in silence for a moment or two, and then Christa opened a door that raised Leila's brows.

"I need to ask you something," she said shyly.

"What is it?" Leila asked, turning to face her.

"If this makes you uncomfortable, please just tell me, but I need to know."

"Spit it out."

"It's about Devon and me."

"Oh no, don't even ask for any inside info about Devon. That, my dear, you are going to have to experience on your own," she said, standing and moving toward the window. Christa loved her view and hardly ever closed the curtains, so she knew why Leila gravitated to Chicago's lakeshore view.

"You're the only person I can ask, and not only that, I know you'll be honest with me," she said, coming over to the window.

"I don't want to get into your and Devon's business. It's freaky enough that you guys somehow hit it off, so no," Leila said, putting up her hands.

"You talk to me all the time about you and Ray."

"You and Ray never hooked up. Or is there something you and Ray failed to mention?" Leila asked, tilting her head to the side and giving Christa her suspicious stare.

"You know that nothing ever happened between us," she said, and the tension in Leila's forehead eased. "All I want to know is one thing," she pleaded, and Leila knew she should not have, but she allowed the question.

"What do you want to know?" she said reluctantly.

"How is Devon in bed?" Christa blurted out, and Leila laughed out loud in her face.

"That is not a question you should be asking me," Leila said, laughing and shaking her head.

"Why not? We're friends."

"And Devon and I were married. I can't discuss our sex life with you."

"You discuss your sex life with me," she said, following Leila back over to the sofa.

"Ummm, hello, that is different. You can't compare the two," she said and flopped down. "This is crazy and so comical, and I'm going to need a shot of something to have this conversation with you. Talking about Ray and me is totally different."

"How we are girlfriends and you tell me about sex with Ray, and I have told you about other guys I've dated, but we can't talk about sex with Devon?"

"Because it's weird. It makes me uncomfortable to think about you and Devon and sex."

"Why? You guys have been over for years now, and you have watched Devon see other women, and you're the only person I can ask," she said, sitting on the ottoman across from Leila and looking at her with desperation in her eyes.

"Why don't you ask Devon? Or better yet, have sex with him? And," Leila added, holding up one finger, "when you do, I don't care to hear about it!" she exclaimed with a serious tone in her voice.

"Are you kidding me?" Christa asked in disbelief.

"I'm serious."

"Well, I will put that in my mental Rolodex, but I can't promise you I won't spill. I wanna have sex with him, but it's like he is afraid to have sex with me."

"Afraid," Leila belted and burst into laughter. "You are so funny, and I haven't laughed this hard in weeks, girl. It may be something, Christa, but fear it isn't. I know Devon way too well. When we were good, the sex was outstanding," Leila said, and then paused, and Christa realized she'd gone back to her original plan of not discussing sex with her ex-husband with Christa.

"So, what can it be?" Christa asked, hoping Leila knew something, because they had been dating for five months, and the only passion they shared were passionate kisses that led them nowhere.

"I don't know."

"Can you find out? Can you talk to him for me, please?" Christa pleaded.

"Are you high? I can't talk to him about why he is not doing you," Leila said, looking at her like she was crazy.

"Come on, Leila, you and Devon are friends, and I really like Devon. I know y'all have some bad history, but you guys are good now, and I know he'll talk to you," Christa said, hoping Leila would help her out.

"Absolutely not. I don't want to get involved or in the middle of your and Devon's sex life. Just talk to him."

"I've tried, but he avoids the conversation. I really like him."

"You are going to have to figure out something, because it's weird enough as it is that you and Devon are together. I do not want to hear a word about you and Devon naked between the sheets or in the shower or on the kitchen counter, you hear me? No matter how hot the story it, I don't wanna hear about it," she said, making it clear.

"Damn, Devon gets down like that?" Christa asked, wondering if that's how he used to do her.

"Eeewww, no, Christa, that is how Rayshon and I do it," she said and laughed.

"Oh shit, I was gonna say," she said, and they both laughed.

"Well, I am not talking about Devon's ass."

"I wish you were," she said and slapped her thigh.

"Give Devon time. He and I do have some bad history, and we went through a very rough patch, but he is a great father, and deep down he is a good person. He just got stupid on me," she said and laughed. "Shit, it wasn't funny back then, but now I'm able to laugh about it."

"I guess you're right," she said and sat there for a moment or two before she went back to Leila's original reason for coming over. "I heard Ray's new spot opened a couple days ago."

"Yep," she replied and smirked a little. "Gym number three."

"That is awesome for you guys. I remember meeting Ray at the old gym he used to work at before he converted his loft. This has always been his dream, and he is doing it."

"Yep, he is," she said, standing to leave. "I'm going to head back to the house. I walked out on Ray after an argument."

"You'll feel better soon. Soon the baby will be here, and you'll have something to do," Christa said, and then wished she hadn't.

"My baby isn't gonna replace my store," Leila said, moving toward the door.

"I know. I didn't mean it that way."

"Thanks for listening. I'll call you tomorrow," Leila said and walked out without giving Christa a chance to say good night.